The Dreadstone King

SIOBHAN MUIR

THREE LAKES BOOKS, LLC

Contents

Published by Three Lakes Books

Cover Design: Furious Fotog

Cover Photographer: Golden Czermak

ISBN: 978-1-947221-31-4

First Print, April 2025

When searching for a relic, be sure there isn't a ghost attached to it...

Reluctance has got nothin' on Allira Maplestaff. She has no interest in participating in the Festival of the Relic, the annual assault on the Dreadstone Tombs to claim the treasure of the Dreadstone King. No one has ever found the relic, won the treasure...or even come back whole. The few who came back alive are tormented shadows of themselves. But to save her grandmothers' farm, she agrees to be the lucky thirteenth warrior to round out the crew.

Josten Ironheart has been dead for over seven decades, but he still detests the annual ritual of sanctioned violence against the residents of the Dreadstone Tombs. He's the Dreadstone King, or at least the ghost of him, and he does his best to drive insane or kill the knights who invade his realm and slaughter his people. When he discovers Allira watching the invaders' horses, he intends to scare her off, but he ends up talking to her...and liking her.

Their friendship continues to grow as the other twelve knights slowly succumb to either their fear or their wounds. But the maniacal leader of the invaders will stop at nothing to claim the relic and the treasure of the Dreadstone Tombs. Josten must protect his home and the woman he loves, but to do that, he must show her his true self. The question is, will Allira be able to see the man beyond the ghost in the skeletal shell?

Dedication

Dedicated to Aerin Varhalmi for the music, for the laughter, and for the plot bunny. This book is all your fault.

Acknowledgments

I know I say this every time, but writing a book is never really a one-person job. There are edits, and proofreading, and formatting, and myriad other nitpicky stuff. Keeping track of details is so much easier when you have help. Not only does it take a great deal of hard work, editing, and research on the part of the author to get things correct, but without my compatriots, there'd be a lot more mistakes.

Great thanks to Susan Sailors for editing this thing. Thanks for reminding me where the pauses are because evidently I don't think of that when writing. Thanks to AKV for proofreading, twice, because the tech wasn't cooperating. Thanks to George Varhalmi for putting this bad boy into Atticus and just making my life easier. And great thanks to Golden Czermak for designing the cover. OMG I swooned just looking at it. And the font? *Chef's kiss*. You rock.

As always, great thanks to my readers for cheering me on. I know you didn't say you needed a fantasy Beauty and the Beast retelling, but here it is. Y'all make my writing worth the detailed effort.

Glossery of Terms in Orkish

Charn – fuck

Dreck – shit

Gronk – idiot, dullard

Gren – Goblin or Orc male

Grell – Goblin or Orc female

Minhra – sweetheart

Swikar – amen

Mada – Honored One

-dri – honorific of respect added to names

The Curse of the Rusty Crown

For those who don the Rusty Crown
It grants the heart's desire
It offers power, wealth, and land
It gives the soul eternal fire.
The Crown picks only those in need,
Who carry the perception of lack,
It offers the wearer the gift of time
To find wealth of heart to give back.
But if the lessons are not quickly learned
And the wearer makes no change,
Then time means nothing, life goes on
And the wearer forever remains.
The Crown's gifts are dearly bought,
It requires atonement in trade,

For all the actions the wearer has wrought
Only in kindness are the debts repaid.

From *The Lesser-Known Cases of Torsha the Bold*
by Torsha Mallesdahtr

13 Knights of the Festival

Sir Milford Argyle

Sir Abel Kettering

Sir Allira Maplestaff

Sir Markus Swindell

Sir Altarman

Sir Barnsworth

Sir Cavanaugh

Sir Craven

Sir Danville

Sir Dinsmore

Sir Hornsby

Sir Tinsley

Sir Wilkerson

Chapter One

*T*his isn't going to go well.

Allira swallowed against the unease as she stood with the horses while four "heroes" prepared to breach the Dreadstone Tombs in search of the Dreastone King's Relic, all in the hopes to buy themselves a bride and a better life. Allira couldn't help the roll of her eyes. Nothing good ever came from 'buying' someone with stolen treasure.

She glanced at the others, taking a breath to tell them it wasn't a good idea. But after the last two weeks of traveling with the group of alternately belligerent and misogynistic knights who'd been chosen for this year's Festival of the Relic, she'd learned her voice meant little. They were each bound and determined to be the one guy who finally found the treasure and claimed the Relic.

Which would be much easier if they even knew what they were looking for.

Nobody did. In fact, in the last three decades of the Festival's run, no one had ever even glimpsed the storied Dreadstone King's Relic, the magical artifact that was supposed to grant the finder something fantastic.

Unfortunately, no one knew what that was, either.

Allira finished tying off the hitching line and checked that each horse was loosely tied to it as the men completed their gear check. She made her way between the horses, loosening girths and making sure nothing dangled off the tack should the men need a quick getaway.

There was rumored to be something horrible in the Dreadstone Tombs, but no one had returned to tell anyone what it was.

Yeah, there's a whole lot we don't *know about this whole fiasco.*

And yet, year after year, men came to Capstone Creek, the nearest settlement to the Dreadstone Tombs at 300 kilometers, and signed up to be one of the lucky 13 Heroes. They were seduced by the legend of gold and riches, and were determined that *this year* they would find the Relic, and win the hand of the princess.

Or one of them would, since there were thirteen of them in all.

Including me.

Except she wasn't going into the Tombs. She had no interest in the treasure, the Relic, *or* the hand of the princess. While she had the skills, the experience as a fighter and warrior, and 'nothing better to do,' she'd been conscripted as the thirteenth warrior to go along by the offer the Village Council and the Magistrate of Capstone Creek had made.

Except she didn't want to go on a fool's errand to raid some creepy tombs for treasure when no one ever came back from them. It was like a reverse virgin sacrifice to a dragon, except it was arrogant and swaggering men with nothing to lose but their lives.

And lose they did. Every year. Every one of them. Perhaps not always physically, but if they did come back, they were broken, haunted, or lost in a fugue state.

Allira groaned and shifted her weight on her feet as she finished with the last horse. There were better ways to be a hero than to raid an old tomb of some guy's junk.

And not the good junk, either.

"Don't forget to watch the horses, nanny goat." Sir Markus Swindell raised his chin so he could look down at her from his 'superior' height of ten extra centimeters above her own.

She gasped. "Oh my goodness, is *that* my job? Thank heavens you reminded me, Swindell, or I just would've gone off by myself." She flattened her expression. "And having a nanny is the only way the lot of you made it out here without losing your way."

He scowled at her sarcasm and turned to the three other men. "Let's go. Treasure awaits."

At least they didn't run screaming into the Tombs' entrance.

No, but they might run screaming out.

She found a nearby boulder and leaned back against it, crossing her arms over her chest. She'd been a fool to take this gig, but helping out her grandmothers without becoming a farmer was too good to pass up.

But since I'm here, I'm not going home to Mima and Nanna, and I won't be able to help them improve our estate.

She could only hope the promises made in exchange for her conscription would be fulfilled and her grandmothers would keep their land, taxes paid in perpetuity. Goddess knew Allira's efforts at being a warrior for hire hadn't paid nearly as much as she'd hoped, even though she was as good or better than the men.

She scowled as old frustrations rose.

The problem was the ones doing the hiring were also men, and they seemed to have tunnel-vision when it came to who they thought were capable at fighting and offering protection. Hell, they'd hire a skinny, pimple-faced green boy who'd never picked up a sword before they'd consider her with her years of experience and capability. It was infuriating.

Almost as infuriating as being conscripted into this stupid quest for prizes she didn't even want.

Despite her credentials, she hadn't been treated as a full warrior by the others. They first tried to treat her as the cook, but she pointed out that they were a team and teams took turns preparing meals. At first, they'd scoffed, but when she said she could easily leave and go back to Capstone Creek, thus making them the unlucky twelve, they backed off insisting she be the sole menial worker.

Well, mostly.

Markus Swindell hadn't let it alone and tried to get the other men to either reduce Allira to their personal squire or the one who made sure camp was set up and clean. It worked the first two nights away from Capstone Creek, but on the third night, she made the remark that only a mama's boy couldn't set up his own tent, care for his own horse, and make his own meal. When they'd bitched, she'd raised her eyebrows and asked why they were supposed to be 'heroes' if they needed someone to help them. It was a wonder they'd ever survived any of their campaigns.

After that, only Markus whined about doing 'woman's work.' She remarked that cooking and cleaning were life skills not wife skills, but obviously they all just needed their nannies. It took a woman to adventure in comfort. But if they wanted to go without, it was none of her business. She was only there to watch the horses. That shut them up quickly.

She climbed up on the boulder and tried to find a comfortable place to sit in the shade of the nearby trees. Staying with the horses kept her out of the creepy dungeons and fulfilled her obligation in exchange for her grandmothers' prosperity.

While the idiots are invading the Tombs under the pretext of treasure and a lost throne.

Yeah, what could go wrong? Allira shook her head and leaned her elbows on her knees. She wished she'd brought a book to read while she was waiting. Instead, she arranged herself comfortably, but easily mobile, and let her eyes unfocus. Maybe she could work on her meditation practices while the idiots got themselves killed.

On the bright side, I might get a few new horses out of the deal.

It wasn't funny even in her head.

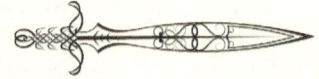

Josten Ironheart waited a few moments more for the warrior to settle herself against the tree behind the boulder before he made his move. The easiest way for him to decrease the number of warriors invading the Dreadstone Caves was to take out their backup and supplies. The problem was he couldn't go far from the arching gates of the entrance so his reach was limited. But the current warrior sat with the horses close enough for him to scare either her or the horses or both.

He threw on his most fearsome aspect—being a decades-old ghost had its advantages—and stepped from the shadows of the gate. The horses' heads came up and their eyes rolled as they took in his skeletal face and hands wrapped in trailing bandages and ragged armor. The iron crown on his head had sharp spikes and seemed massive compared to his skull, a grim visage that had frightened many warriors in the past.

But the warrior on the boulder didn't stir, her eyes closed as if she slept. Upright.

What is she doing?

She was totally ruining his approach, and he stopped, waiting for her to open her eyes.

She took a few deep breaths and resettled her body into an upright position, before breathing out slowly. She sat there for several minutes, and he waited, ready to use his fear tactic to the best of his ability.

But the time dragged on longer than he could ever remember it flowing, and he grew frustrated. He considered spooking the horses to get a reaction, but the poor beasts weren't at fault and it was rather petulant to use them just for her attention.

Finally, she sighed and threw her hands out. "I should've brought a damn book."

He jumped, surprised that she spoke aloud, and scurried back into the shadows before she saw him.

So much for being the Dreadstone King, Demon of the Deeps, Killer of Heroes, and Keeper of the Secrets.

He rolled his eyes at himself. If anyone knew the truth behind the Dreadstone Caves, they wouldn't send men to search for treasure every year, insisting they'd win riches and a throne. No one had ever succeeded in taking either, for decades. There were riches, but he hadn't accumulated them while he was alive. They were brought by the other denizens of the caves, mostly for decoration, since neither the dead nor the Goblins, Orcs, Trolls, Ghouls, Nagas, and bats put much value in the gold or jewels.

As for himself, he'd once wanted such things, and when he'd first come to the Dreadstone Caves, his intent had been to make his fortune and become a king. And he had, thinking himself better than others and worthy of everyone's adulation.

But then he came into possession of the Iron Crown—a great spiked circlet with polished points on each spike—and once he placed it on his head, it possessed his soul, holding it in the world even when Death came to take him. Josten had been bound to the crown and couldn't leave, stuck with his useless throne and kingdom of dread for all eternity.

If he'd been left alone, it might have been lonely but tolerable. But someone in the human communities far from the caves had decided they were a prize to be conquered and won. Thus started the Festival of the Relic—a contest for any and all eligible 'heroes' to search the Dreadstone Tombs, as they called them, for the Relic and win themselves a kingdom and riches. He'd heard some of the intruders this year say there was also a princess in the prize package.

I wonder if anyone asked her if she was okay with being the consort of the Dreadstone King?

Over the last thirty years, only five 'heroes' had ever encountered the Relic and survived, but they all went mad when having to face Josten in his flaming death aspect, and they fled. Josten remained ruling over Dreadstone.

And now I'm looking at yet another year of contestants in the 'wanna-die-young-or-crazy' game.

If he didn't run away from the one warrior sitting outside the caves.

"This is ridiculous, you know that?"

The woman's voice cut across the space before the gate, her irritation plain.

Is she talking to me?

Josten let go of his visible aspect and peered around the trees. She'd dropped from the boulder and paced in front of the horses, her scowl perfectly etched on her freckled face. She had a full head of short, dark hair held back from her face with an oxblood-red cloth band. Her eyes were pale, but he couldn't tell what color as she strode along the line of horses, checking gear for something to do.

"No one should be stupid enough to go into the Tombs. Hell, I bet there's nothing actually in there except other dead idiots and the occasional spider." She threw her hands out. "I didn't even want to be here, but they needed thirteen warriors for a lucky number so here I am." She scowled up at the sky. "I'm only doing this for my grandmothers!"

Josten shot a look around the clearing, but found only trees and horses. He returned his gaze to her frustrated features, and his curiosity stirred. Despite her agitation, she was gentle with the animals, carefully inspecting their tack and checking their feet for stones. Maybe he wouldn't scare her. Maybe he'd just talk to her.

He snorted. Whoever heard of the Dreadstone King, a man long dead but stuck in a twilight existence because of his lust for riches and power, just talking to someone? That smacked of loneliness.

He damn near laughed aloud. The Dreadstone King, lonely? How absurd.

Except, it felt true, and the bleak, desolate centuries of solitude loomed ahead of him. His heart shriveled a little more.

What heart? I'm nothing more than a ghost and a skeleton with a crown.

The old fury and frustration rose in his chest, and a howl broke loose. The horses spooked and the warrior whipped around, drawing her sword as her body tensed for action. But he hurtled himself back through the gate into the Dreadstone Tombs, hounded by his own recriminations. He'd take his frustrations out on the latest batch of invaders and watch them scream in terror.

Chapter Two

It took twenty minutes to grab all the horses and calm them down after Allira ascertained there wasn't a threat. To be honest, her own heart had shot out of her chest when the howl ripped through the forest, and it had taken her several seconds to figure out what had happened. Then she swore and rushed to try to untangle the horses as their tack had slipped off their backs and made a mess.

She'd finally calmed them all and got them tacked up just as the men ran out of the entrance to the Tombs. Though she had never been there before, she could tell it was a freaky place that probably should be left alone. Only three of the four men who'd gone in came bolting for the horses. Their faces were whiter than a burial shroud, and none of them were joking anymore.

"What happened? Where's Danville?" Allira released the tether rope holding the horses' leads. She caught her mount and

Danville's, but no one answered her as they kicked their mounts into a gallop.

Allira paused, holding the horses still as she turned back to the Tombs, scanning for the last knight to come out. His horse tugged at the reins, trying to follow the others, but she forced it to wait.

Come on, Danville. Where are you?

But after ten minutes, he still hadn't appeared, and she realized he wouldn't be coming. The Tombs had claimed its first hero of the year. A combination of anger and disgust settled into her belly as she swung up into the saddle and turned from the Tombs, tugging Danville's horse behind her. What a stupid, fucking waste. The only thing the Tombs brought was death and despair for families.

Allira rode back to camp and tried to find something good about the day.

Make a list, minhra. Her Mima's voice echoed in her thoughts. *List all the good things so you may count your blessings, even in times of strife.*

She ground her teeth as she rode into camp, trying to ignore the men who were picking over Danville's possessions like vultures at a corpse. She claimed his horse and figured it would provide a relief mount for her own. She paused at her tent and slid off Javalina, her gray roan. The horse eyed Danville's bay mare, but settled down as soon as Allira took their tack off and fed them.

"Hey, Allira. What makes you think you can keep Danville's horse?" Markus sneered as he carried off Danville's extra weapons.

"Let me think." She tilted her head like a coquette as she ticked off her fingers. "I took care of it all day. I waited for him at the entrance to the Tombs. I took it with me when I left the Tombs. Sounds like ownership to me." She gave him a patently false smile. "The horse and her tack are mine." She rested one hand on her dagger. "Got a problem with that?"

He scowled but said nothing as he continued on to his tent.

"I thought not." She turned back to the horses and brushed them down before settling in to piece together a meal of dried meat and corn cakes. She didn't trust these men any farther than she could throw them, so she ate facing the community fire without joining them.

Most of the men boasted about how many creatures they'd killed in the Tombs, never admitting to those who hadn't been there how they'd run out with their faces white and their tails between their buttocks. Allira snorted. She wasn't going to give away their secrets, but she knew the truth. They'd been terrified, running for their lives.

At least they didn't run screaming.

She didn't blame them for running—apparently, they'd invaded someone's home and that someone defended themselves with prejudice. She hadn't expected the Tombs to be occupied, but it sounded as if there were Orcs and Goblins living in the Tombs.

And these jackasses are boasting about killing them.

Of course, she wasn't much different. She was there, to 'win the treasure of the Tombs' because they'd needed a thirteenth member.

I should've said no.

But it was too late to back out now and she had to see it through. *But I'm not going inside those damn Tombs.* No, she'd be content to stay outside with the horses who were far better company than the men who rode them. And she could meditate and listen to the birds in the trees.

"On the morrow, we start going in as teams of two so no one's left behind." Swindell was blathering on about the next day's excursion. "It's safer to use the buddy-system."

Allira snorted. *As if he didn't leave Danville in the dust the moment he could get away.*

The other men nodded and murmured assent.

"Except for Allira. She'll watch over the horses like she did today." He smirked at her from across the fire.

She shrugged. "Works for me. They're better company anyway."

One of the others laughed. "She's got you there, Swindell. You always were more of a horse's arse."

"Shut up, Cavanaugh. You spend all your time dreaming about her arse to notice the rest of us." Swindell smirked and grabbed his groin. "Maybe we should give you a chance at her, eh?"

Allira's heart sped up, but she pulled out her knife and started cleaning her fingernails.

"Anyone who comes into my tent at night will find themselves with a hole in their thigh deep enough to bleed out and the distinct possibility of losing what balls they have." She shrugged nonchalantly even though unease tickled the back of her neck. "I'm here because *you* need *me*, not because I wanted to be here. So, take those chips off your shoulders, boys. I'm not here to steal your glory, or your treasure. Leave me alone and we won't have problems. Hear me?"

She kept cleaning her nails, but she met everyone's gaze and more than one of the knights looked away. Only Swindell held her gaze and smirked. Allira resigned herself to cat-napping that night, with her dagger in her hands.

The next morning, she woke almost as tired as she'd gone to bed, but she'd been left alone and she still had Danville's horse, so she counted herself lucky. She'd have to devise a warning system of bells or bits of broken chainmail to make noise when someone tried to come into her tent.

Because she wouldn't put it past Swindell to try to take her out if he thought she was doing better than him.

A good possibility since I won't be going into the Tombs.

She rose and put together a small pot with water to boil over the communal fire. Fortunately, she was almost the first one up and made her meal fast enough to be gone by the time the rest of the knights staggered to the fire.

Once she'd finished eating, she took a few moments to look at the remains of Danville's things. The others had taken pretty much everything but the tent and a few knickknacks. Even the stuffed grass pallet he'd used to sleep on was gone. But there was a small pile of personal items the others hadn't found valuable. There were two leather-bound journals, a pencil nub, and a rubbing cloth to erase mistakes.

Allira picked them up and opened the journals. One was blank, but the other had daily entries from the last year or so written in a small, precise hand. Mostly he talked about his experiences with training and fighting others, but she found a few entries that read more like letters to someone. She closed the journal before she could read more and carried both back to her tent.

Maybe there's a way to get the full journal to his loved ones when we get back.

If any of them made it back to the village alive. Given what happened to Danville, it looked less and less likely.

"All right, men, let's mount up." Swindell's voice echoed across the camp, and she groaned.

She hadn't packed up her midday meal yet. From the looks of things, the others weren't quite ready to leave either, so she put together her gear while the others complained to Markus to hold his horses. She packed the extra journal to have something to do while she watched the horses, and saddled up Javalina in time to ride out after the six-man invasion force.

Lucky number seven, I guess.

When she got to the clearing before the gate, she found the horses tied to various trees, some with their hind feet already cocked in relaxation. Allira shook her head and gathered each horse, clipping it to the semi-permanent picket line she'd strung up their first day.

Men! Always needing a woman to clean up after them.

She loosened the tack on the horses, lengthened their leads so they could get their heads to the ground, and settled in for a long boring wait for the 'triumphant' return of panicked knights. She pulled out the empty journal and the pencil nub and started writing her observations of the whole fiasco called the Festival of the Relic.

The day stretched, and the forest sounds came to life the longer the men were gone. The sun broke through the morning mist and painted dappled shadows on the Tombs' gate. Allira took a few moments to study the shifting shapes as the wind blew through the trees, clearing away the wisps of fog. She loved this time of year when the world got ready to settle down into the harvest months. Her grandmothers would preserve fruit and make jams and breads to give away around Samhain.

And instead of helping them, I'm stuck here watching horses for a bunch of numbskulls.

She shook her head and rolled her eyes, but as she did, she caught something out of the corner of her eye and whipped her head around. A man stood in the shadows of the gate, observing her. He had dark brown hair that hung around his face in shoulder-length waves and a matching beard. He wore leather armor stained a deep oxblood red over chainmail and a black and gold doublet belted to his waist with a long dagger at his side.

He appeared to be waiting for her to notice him as he leaned back against the gate, his arms in leather bracers crossed over his chest.

Allira scrambled to her feet but kept her hands off her weapons. He hadn't made any aggressive moves, but she didn't want to be on her ass when he chose to move.

For a moment, neither of them said anything, and she wondered who he was. He wasn't one of this year's crop of knights, but he didn't look worn and grizzled like anyone from previous years. He looked young, fit, capable, and seasoned without being old.

"Good morning. Can I help you?"

That seemed like as good an opener as any, though she wasn't sure how she could help someone who looked at home near the Tombs.

He laughed, though it never reached his pale green eyes. "I believe that's my question."

She blinked. "Do I look like I need help?"

He shrugged. "Maybe not, but usually all the warriors who come to this place are looking for something."

"Oh." She scowled and nodded. "Yeah, that's not really my thing. I'm just watching the horses."

He raised his eyebrows in disbelief. "You're just here to watch the horses?"

She nodded. "Yup."

"Have you no interest in the treasure of the Tombs?"

She shook her head. "Nope."

He scoffed. "I find that hard to believe. Aren't you a warrior yourself?"

She tilted her head. "Oh yeah, I'm definitely a warrior, but I'm not interested in entering the Tombs. That's for idiots and fools."

He laughed again, this time with more amusement. "Strange sentiment for a warrior with a short sword on one hip and a long dagger on the other."

She shrugged. "The best warriors know when to avoid a fool's errand." She narrowed her eyes. "Who are you?"

The knight hesitated. "I'm called Josten."

"Josten." An old name but not that uncommon among the landed gentry in Capstone Creek. Odd he hadn't used a family surname. "What brings you all the way out here? I don't recall you being part of this year's crop."

He raised his eyebrows. "Crop?"

She grimaced. "Yeah, crop of idiots set to go into the Tombs after the mythical treasure that's supposed to be there. You know, the Festival of the Relic."

"Ah yes, I've heard of that. Do they really believe they'll find anything valuable?"

She snorted and waved at the horses. "I didn't just show up with several horses just to hang out in the shade. So, I know you're not from this year's festival. Do you live nearby?"

He gave her a rueful smirk. "Something like that. Who are you, Warrior-who-won't-enter?"

She tilted her head. "Allira Maplestaff."

He raised his eyebrows. "That's it? No titles or regions to go with your name?"

"Nope."

Josten waited expectantly for her to say more, but that was all she had. "Truly?"

"Yup."

He laughed. "Very well. It's good to meet you, Allira. What do you do out here while the others go traipsing around in the Tombs?"

She grinned. "Traipsing is an interesting choice of words to describe six manchildren searching for glory and supposed treasure by entering a place they have no business being. I thought they were more of 'invading' the Tombs. I'm sure the Orcs and Goblins think so."

His eyebrows went up again. "You care what the Orcs and Goblins think?"

She shrugged. "Kinda. I mean, I didn't know there were any people in the Tombs. The name kinda suggests they're empty. But if it was my home and I was minding my own business, I wouldn't want anyone to invade just because they thought I had items of value. The Orcs and Goblins don't bother anyone as far as I can tell, and these jerks invade their home once a year to take away their collection of gold and jewels—at least I assume it's gold and jewels. It could just be a large collection of vintage spider silk."

Josten smirked. "Vintage spider silk?"

"Yeah, you know, decades of spider webs. I'm sure you get enough of them and they become valuable to someone." She grinned. "Not that I don't find them valuable, but I have no interest in scouring the Tombs for them just to find out."

"And just think how the spiders would react when someone takes their supply." Josten smirked.

"Oh yeah, that could be bad." She shuddered theatrically. "So, what brings you to the gate of the Dreadstone Tombs?"

He shrugged. "I saw the horses and wondered what they were doing here. Then I saw you."

"And you just had to say hello."

He nodded. "Something like that."

"Well then, hello, Josten." She waved at him, and to her delight, he waved back.

"Hello. May I join you since you're just waiting here for..." He frowned a moment and swung his gaze around the entrance. "What *are* you waiting for?"

Allira sighed. "The current team of idiots who've invaded the Tombs today." She waved at the gate. "They're sure they'll discover the treasure—the same treasure *no one* has found in at least thirty years since the Festival began—and they needed someone to watch the horses. So I volunteered to stay out here. There's probably something here to keep me entertained while I wait for them." She waved at the horses again. "I should probably go through their saddlebags to see."

"Perhaps I could keep you company until they return so you're not so bored."

She raised her eyebrows. "Don't you have something better to do than sit out here waiting for the young and the clueless?"

"I can think of nothing better to do than chat with you."

Allira laughed. "That's a helluva line you got there, Josten."

He sighed and leaned against a tree nearby. "Not a line. Just the truth."

She lowered her brows and narrowed her eyes. "What do you normally do all day when I'm not here?"

He shrugged and his lips tightened for a moment. "Mostly it's maintenance and yardwork. Chores."

"Ugh, yeah, I know that routine." She nodded. "If I'm not at my grandmothers' place helping take care of the livestock and garden, I'm at home making sure my weapons and armor are in top condition."

He moved to a rock closer to her boulder and leaned back on his hands. "Your parents have a farm? How did you become a warrior, then?"

Allira snorted. "My grandparents, but I wasn't cut out to be a farmer. It's hard work, but it's always the same, day in and day out. Some people really like the routine—it brings them comfort knowing there won't be many surprises. But I couldn't do it. I needed a challenge that gave me purpose beyond feeding animals and tilling the soil."

He nodded. "I completely understand. My family were farmers, too, and I learned the hardship of the daily grind."

"Right? It's totally exhausting. I'd rather drill all day than do the backbreaking work of tilling the ground year after year." She shot him a smile. "How did you get out of the farm life?"

"Honestly? I ran away when I was old enough to hold a sword and do more than cut grasses with it." He grimaced and glanced down at his hands. "I met up with a band of mercenaries who took pity on me and let me be their general squire—essentially an errand boy who tended to their gear. But in exchange, they fed me and taught me how to fight with weapons and hand-to-hand."

"Mercenaries, huh? Not really the traditional path to knight-hood."

"No, but it taught me a lot about people, their motivations, and who to trust. It served me well." He shrugged.

"Which group of mercenaries? I know of a few bands, but haven't trained with any of them." She pulled the dagger from her belt and held it out to Josten. "I won this dagger off one of the Carpathia's Crusaders lieutenants. I was a lot younger then and they thought I was too green to be on the field with them. So, they challenged me to a wrestling match to keep our weapons honed." She shrugged with a smug smile. "I beat him. Of course, he didn't know I'd been helping my grandmothers wrestle and shear sheep for years, and they're a lot stronger and more squirmy."

Josten laughed. "I wish I could've seen that. I bet he didn't know what hit him."

"Nope. He lost fair and square, so he had to give up his dagger." She waved it with a grin before shoving it into its scabbard. "So, which mercs were you with?"

Josten looked toward the gate to the Tombs, his jaw suddenly tight. "The Wraiths."

"Shiiiiiiittt." Allira breathed out the word. "Those guys were badass and crazy to boot."

He nodded. "They were."

She frowned a moment, searching her memories. "Didn't they all die out or disband or something after a huge fight?"

Josten sighed, and deep regret filled his voice. "Yes, they did."

Chapter Three

Sorrow and regret filled Josten's chest as he remembered the last time he'd fought with the Wraiths. It was the day he became the Dreadstone King. The day his ego got the better of him and he lost the first bit of his humanity.

Dreck, it's been almost a hundred and thirty years.

Still, that didn't seem to be enough time to get over the hurt he'd caused to the family that had given him a chance to be more than just a farm boy stuck in the dirt. But the lure of riches, no fighting, and the chance to live by no one's rules but his own were too much to resist. He broke with the Wraiths, claimed the treasure of the Dreadstone Tombs as his own, and ruled for sixty-five brutal years until the cost became clear.

He couldn't die.

Not in the true sense of the word.

His body had withered into nothing but an articulated skeleton held together by some sort of magical strands that held each bone in place. But the spirit was tied to the bones by the spiked crown of twisted iron, lacquered in black paint, except for the points which now sat heavy in rust. The crown itself wasn't particularly valuable for its parts, but the magic held in the metal granted the wearer great power and treasure.

The only drawback was it also kept the wearer's soul—forever—until the next person found it and took it from the current owner. Josten had taken it off the head of a skeleton seated on the throne in the caves. He'd laughed at the warning from his mentors in the Wraiths, wanting the treasure and the power more than anything else.

So they left him, moving on, doing jobs for anyone who needed a military force, and Josten built his kingdom. He hadn't done it with kindness or justice, but he had ruled, and for a while there was relative peace.

But the Wraiths returned some twenty years later, claiming they'd heard rumors of Josten's ruthlessness. They begged him to reconsider leaving the treasure and the throne, or taking on advisors who could help him become a better king than he'd been.

But with the crown affixed to his head, and its dark, angry magic surging through him, he accused the Wraiths of trying to usurp his power, and he sent his army out to destroy them.

None of them survived. And he lost the last of his humanity with their deaths.

He'd only ruled—alive—sixty years more before the crown had stolen too much of his soul and his body died. Those held in thrall were released and fled, and the Dreadstone Kingdom became the Dreadstone Caves. Josten ruled over stone, gold, jewels, and silence.

Until the looters came to take the gold and jewels, spreading the word far and wide about the Dreadstone treasure. But after there was nothing left of value to the humans, the Goblins, Orcs, Ghouls, and finally the Nagas filled the rooms left beneath the vaulted ceilings and stalactites. They claimed the spaces for homes away from humans, and built their own communities, leaving his skeleton seated on the throne he'd valued.

"I'm sorry for your loss."

Josten blinked. "What?"

"The loss of the Wraiths. They were your friends and family, right?" Allira shot him a compassionate look.

He sighed. "Yes, they were. And far wiser than I knew until it was too late." He glanced down at his ghostly hands and scowled. One day, he'd be free of his curse, and he could join the Wraiths in the afterlife, apologizing for his stupidity.

But today wasn't the day.

He rose to his feet and spun to face her. "I'm sorry, Sir Allira, but I must leave you. Chores to complete before the day is done. Thank you for the conversation and maybe I'll see you in the coming days."

Disappointment shadowed her expression until she shrugged. "Oh, I'll be here. This farce doesn't end until someone finds the Dreadstone Treasure or they all die trying."

"Won't that mean you'll automatically win the contest?"

She shook her head. "Nope. I only win if I get the treasure, which I don't want, by going in the place I don't want to visit, and then they'll give me the hand of the princess, who I don't want to marry. So, really, it's lose-lose for me."

"Then why *are* you here?" Josten couldn't imagine wasting so much time.

She shrugged. "As I said, I'm doing this for my grandmothers so they can keep their land without fuss. Once this farce is over, I can go on to do my own thing."

Despite his need to get away from his wretched memories, he tilted his head. "And what's the thing you want to do?"

She opened her mouth to reply, but the words seemed to stick in her throat. After a few moments, she blew her breath out in frustration. "No fucking clue."

A surprised laugh burst out of him. "So things are going to plan, then?" He grinned. "The good news is you'll have plenty of time to think about it while your compatriots are in the Tombs raiding for treasure."

"They're not my *compatriots*. They're just the egocentric idiots I was conscripted to accompany." She rolled her eyes. "But you're right—I'll have plenty of time to think of what I'm going to do when they either find this mythical treasure or die trying."

"What happens when they all die? What will you do then?"

She smirked. "Well, I'll at least have a large herd of warhorses. Maybe I'll set up a riding stable where kids can come for birthday parties, and war horsey rides."

Josten laughed again. "That's not a bad idea. Can adults do that too?"

"I don't see why not. I mean, they might have to wear paper hats and brightly colored tabards with 'Birthday Boy' embroidered on them, but sure." Allira shrugged, her eyes sparkling with humor.

"I think you could make a true business out of that." His grin stretched his face enough to tire the muscles. "You should think it over, but I really must go. Will I see you tomorrow?"

"Yup. Same place, same time, same horses." She shrugged.

"I'll be here." And he was surprised to realize he meant the words completely.

Allira watched Josten disappear into the trees with a bemused smile.

What the hell had just happened?

When had hanging out with a bunch of horses and chit-chatting with some random guy been her thing? Of course, most of the time she was around men was either when they were in a fighting team, or this fiasco where she wasn't with them at all. It was refreshing to spend time with a guy who just seemed to be interested in hanging out.

Still, it was weird that he'd just appeared out of nowhere. As far as she knew, there were no villages or dwellings within a fortnight's ride of the Dreadstone Tombs. So where had he come from?

It's not like I've mapped the whole area, though.

True, she hadn't, and someone like Josten could've built a place to live nearby without anyone else knowing about it. If the Goblins, Orcs, and other cave dwellers didn't mind, she certainly couldn't begrudge him his solitary existence.

Maybe she could do some exploring while the men went into the Tombs. It wasn't like they needed her for anything, and when they came boiling out at the end of the day, they weren't much for talking. Hell, she might want to move her own camp away from the others. Survival training maintained that two were one, and one was none, but she couldn't help but feel she might be safer in the shadow of the Dreadstone Tombs than she was with the other human men.

She mulled over the idea of breaking camp, but decided she'd ask Josten about it the next day.

If he indeed shows up again.

Strangely, she hoped he would. She'd enjoyed sharing her time with him and he'd been interesting to talk to. Better than just sitting there watching the trees grow. Or listening to the horses snore. She glanced at the leather notebook and grimaced.

I guess I could write more observations down.

She rose and stretched then wandered over to Javalina to check his tack. Her gut said the men would be coming out soon, and she wanted to be ready to head back to camp. She kinda liked the idea of packing up and camping elsewhere, but she didn't want to intrude on Josten's solitude.

"Still, he was pretty friendly for someone who lives alone, wasn't he, Javalina?"

The gray roan nudged her shoulder and lipped at her hand, looking for treats. She laughed and wished she had an apple to give him, but she rubbed his neck and checked his bridle for fit. She glanced at the sun and grimaced. The men should be coming out soon, but that meant they'd either be disappointed or scared, and she wasn't in the mood to deal with any of them.

I've had a fortnight of dealing with them and I'm done.

The idea of going back to camp with the knights filled her with dread. There was something off about some of them, Swindell in particular, but none of them were trustworthy as far as her safety was concerned.

Except for Danville. And he was dead. She glanced at the bay. *Thanks for the packhorse, Danville.*

She checked the sun again. Maybe it was a good time to head to camp and pack her shit on Danville's horse while they were still in the Tombs. She could make camp elsewhere and not have to worry who might be trying to ambush her. She already knew what these men would do when they wanted something.

The Goblins and Orcs know, too.

But where could she settle? She couldn't assume Josten would be cool with her intrusion into his lands. She scanned the line of horses. She couldn't leave them to be prey for whatever lived nearby. If anything happened to the animals, the men would lose their minds and blame her. She sighed and scowled at the gates. She'd just have to make it one more night with the knights and see what Josten said the next day.

I'd rather sleep near the Goblins and Orcs.

Despite the looming night with the creep brigade, the idea of camping somewhere in Josten's land brought her a measure of peace and hope.

Chapter Four

T he day at the Tombs had been more disastrous to the knights than usual. While only one died, another was grievously wounded and couldn't ride out the next day. After squabbling over who got the dead knight's horse and gear, the men stated that Allira should stay behind to nurse the wounded knight because 'of her womanly skills.'

She snorted. "I thought you men have been on the field of battle before. You don't have any skills to take care of the wounded or sick?" She shook her head. "Then a lot of you are going to die fast. I'm just here to make sure your numbers were lucky and to look after the horses. Unless you want to leave them to the predators?"

When no one could answer, she told them to draw straws on who'd care for the wounded and retreated to her tent.

The men stayed up and drank to the dead knight, though no one could quite remember his name. The others who'd survived bragged about all the Orcs they'd killed as they swilled their drinks.

Allira gritted her teeth and made sure both her sword and her dagger were within reach.

She took a few moments to write her thoughts about Josten in the leather journal. He'd been surprisingly good company. While he was similar to the knights she'd come with, he carried himself with a surety of purpose and experience. He was confident without being cocky, dangerous without being threatening, and knowledgeable without being arrogant.

And being handsome doesn't hurt either.

Unlike with the other knights, she didn't have to be on her guard all the time when with him. She hadn't realized how much of a comfort that was until she thought about going back to camp with the others.

She wrinkled her nose as she put her journal in her pack. The men outside were still bragging and drinking, and she wondered how they were going to raid the next day with their hangovers. She closed up her tent, tying the flap securely from the inside, and settled into her bedroll, still dressed, with her dagger in its sheath. She touched her sword to make sure it remained beside her and closed her eyes.

Allira jolted awake and slid her hand over the hilt of her dagger. Something was wrong.

She froze and held her breath, waiting to see which way to move in either defense or attack. It was dark without the fire's glow, and the wind ruffled the trees around the clearing where they'd camped. But her tent moved in an odd way and she could hear heavy breathing and muttering. Someone fumbled at opening the front flap to get inside.

She snarled silently and pushed back the blankets as she sat up. She grasped her sword and pulled it slowly from the scabbard, making as much noise as possible, an unmistakable sound of metal against leather.

The fumbling and muttering stopped, and all she could hear was the heavy breathing.

"You keep trying to get into my tent, and you won't have a cock or balls left to be found in the morning. I will gut you and leave your corpse for the vultures to pick over." She growled the words just loud enough for her would-be assailant to hear.

She waited for the drunkard to make a decision, her hand tightening on her hilt. The wind kept rustling, but her tent remained still until she heard a groan and stumbling steps moving away. She let her breath out slowly and closed her eyes, listening to her racing heart.

No question about it. I'm fucking moving my camp.

She'd pack her shit in the morning. She just hoped Josten would be okay with her moving closer because she'd fucking pick the Orcs over staying with the men.

In the morning, Allira was up before everyone else simply because she couldn't sleep after the threat of assault. She'd packed up all her gear, left it in her tent, and sat eating a meal by the time the men got up. She watched them to see if anyone gave indication of his guilt at trying her tent, but no one looked in her direction.

She scanned the faces. Who was the creep who'd tried to get into her tent? No one looked particularly guilty, though several of them looked like they'd been hit over the head with a board. She narrowed her eyes, but couldn't tell which one of them to be wary of most.

Which means all of them are threats.

Finally, Swindell declared that he and five others would ride out. The last three would be required to care for the wounded knight, and Allira would be on horse duty.

"Maplestaff, did you hear me?" Swindell's voice broke through her thoughts.

"Yup, got it. Horse duty. Acknowledged." She nodded and took a sip of her tea.

"Are you coming?"

She raised her eyebrows. "I'll be there soon. What's the hurry? The picket line is still there, and you can tie your horses off. I'll be on my way when I'm ready."

"Yeah, Swindell. Let up on her, eh? It's not like the horses are really going anywhere, and she won't be long."

Another knight, she thought his name might be Wilkerson, waved off Swindell and gave her a friendly wink. She didn't react, but suspicions rose in her mind as she bit into an apple. Was he the guy who'd tried her tent the night before? None of them had ever tried being nice or friendly to her, and his timing seemed suspect.

Swindell scowled. "Don't take too long. Just do your damned job." He reined his horse over roughly and rode off with the others in a huff.

Wilkerson rolled his eyes. "So fucking full of himself."

Allira didn't react, still wondering at Wilkerson's motivation.

Sir Abel Kettering joined them at the fire and shot her a reproachful look. "You should be more friendly and smile more. It'll make it easier for you."

Allira shot him a considering look. "You should try to be more kind and gentle, but I don't see that happening anytime soon."

Kettering drew himself up to look down his nose at her. "I'm kind. My mother says so."

"Oh, well, in that case, since she *says so*, I shall just have to revise my view." She scrunched up her nose and squinted, before sighing and shaking her head. "Nope, view not revised."

Wilkerson laughed as she rose and tossed the apple core into the fire before heading to her tent with her dishes, more determined to pack her stuff on Danville's bay and get the flock out of camp.

She didn't talk to the other knights, but she kept an eye on them as she loaded her gear onto the packhorse. Most of the men joked quietly with each other or tended the wounded, and didn't pay her much attention. The creep in the night hadn't said anything so she couldn't tell by voice who it was, but all of them smelled like alcohol and none of them mentioned not sleeping well.

Allira packed up the last of her things except her tent so no one would notice the change until the last moment. Once the load, minus the tent, sat balanced on Danville's bay, she struck the tent and added it to the back of Javalina's saddle, still keeping an eye on the men.

"All right, Foxtrot." She patted the bay. "I promise you won't be used as a packhorse for very long. Just until I find a new place—a safer place—to camp."

Foxtrot nosed her hands, looking for the apple she'd been eating.

"Sorry, big girl. I'll try to save the core for you next time."

She patted the horse and checked all the bindings before swinging up into Javalina's saddle. She turned the horses toward the path to the Tombs, but Sir Kettering stood and stepped into her way.

"Where the hell are you going?" Kettering stuffed his beefy hands on his hips.

She raised an eyebrow. "Is this some sort of trick question? I'm following Swindell's orders to start watching the horses while the big boys go play in the Tombs." She gestured toward the trail out of camp. "You gonna get out of my way?"

He scowled. "You're going with all your gear?"

She shrugged. "Yeah. You never know what you might need while sitting around doing nothing."

Wilkerson joined him and frowned. "Are you leaving?"

"I'm going to the clearing outside the Tombs. Why is this a surprise?"

Wilkerson gestured to Foxtrot. "You're taking a packhorse full of your gear."

Nothing gets past you.

"I think I'll camp closer to the Tombs. There's no point in riding back and forth since I'm not really needed here and I'm not making forays into the caverns." *And I won't have to deal with you.* She kept the last to herself.

"What do you mean you're not needed here?" Wilkerson crossed his arms over his chest, and his expression grew uneasy.

"You're going to camp *closer* to the Tombs? Are you completely daft?" Sir Milford Argyle gaped at her as he looked up from helping the injured knight drink some water.

"Nope. The Tombs don't bother me. They're actually fairly serene—"

"Aye, but that's during the day, lass. You'll be Naga-fodder at night, you will." Argyle shook his russet brown head, the braids in his long hair and beard swinging with his disbelief. "Who will protect you then?"

Protect me from whom?

"Aww, are you worried about me, Sir Argyle? I'm touched." She reined Javalina around Kettering and Wilkerson. "I can protect myself. I'll be fine, and you'll have your horse guard. Be sure to keep looking after the injured. See you at the Tombs when it's your turn."

She rode away from the sputtering knights, but again wondered at their motives. She listened hard for any signs of pursuit because she didn't trust that they'd just let her go. But once she was well out of camp, her shoulders relaxed. She'd escaped before anything awful had happened and now she had the opportunity to find a safe place to camp.

If Josten's good with it.

Her sense of relief gave way to uncertainty. She'd only met the guy and talked to him once. That didn't mean he'd be fine with her moving into his domain. She hoped he wouldn't send her back to the camp of the invaders. Not only would it be embarrassing, it would also put her in constant danger. Because she had no doubt the drunkard would try again another night.

She swallowed against her misgivings and rode toward the clearing where they left the horses.

The clearing sat quiet with the abandoned horses tied to the picket line, their girths still tight against their bellies. Allira rolled her eyes and pulled Javalina up beside them. She tied her ride to a tree and went to check on the others, loosening girths and checking their hooves for rocks. She used a stick to dislodge the few stones then returned to check on Javalina and Foxtrot.

Biting her lip, she scanned the clearing. Josten hadn't arrived, but she didn't want to unsaddle either horse until she had an answer from him about her accommodations. But she couldn't leave them tacked up all day, especially Foxtrot with all her belongings.

She glanced at the Tombs, wondering when Josten would show up. He'd said he would, but sometimes life got in the way of intentions. She sighed and loosened her horses' girths, but left the tack on their backs. They could handle it for a couple of hours, and she expected Josten well before that.

I hope.

At least this time she had the journal with her. That should keep her occupied until Josten arrived. She settled in the shade on a flat stone and opened the journal, but she couldn't think of anything she wanted to write. She frowned and shifted position, turning her back to the gate. But her mind kept drifting to the near-assault the night before and if Josten would allow her to camp nearby. She just kept looking around the clearing, in hopes of spying Josten.

Ugh! I'm being ridiculous.

She rose and stretched, stuffing the journal back into her things as she tried to calm her mind enough to settle. She rolled her head on her shoulders and stretched her arms this way and that, but it didn't help her relax. With a groan of frustration, she yanked out her sword and threatened a nearby tree. She pretended it was one of the knights and went to work on fighting formations. That helped her focus, and muscle memory kicked in. Her mind settled into the well-known patterns, and she flowed seamlessly from one workout to another.

By the time she'd worked up a good sweat and her muscles were begging to stop, Allira caught sight of Josten leaning against his favorite tree, his expression intent.

"Glory! Josten. I didn't see you. When did you get here?" She shoved the sword back into its scabbard and retreated to Javalina to grab a rag to wipe the sweat off her face.

"Long enough to know you're quite skilled."

She snorted. "You sound surprised. Did you think I was lying to you when I said I was a warrior?"

He grimaced and shrugged one shoulder. "It's just unusual to find a woman who's as skilled as most male warriors."

She rolled her eyes. "Actually, it's a lot more common than you think. Contrary to popular belief, males aren't the best warriors nor do they have the most skill."

He didn't say anything, as if he waited for her to add some sort of caveat to her statement. She instead turned to grab her waterskin.

He cleared his throat and looked around as if searching for something to say. "It was more unusual back in my time. The Wraiths didn't employ many women."

She frowned, trying to remember how long ago the Wraiths were a feared group. She remembered her grandmothers talking about them when they were children, but not since her own parents had been born.

It has to be over sixty years ago.

Seemed weird that he spoke about the Wraiths as if he'd been with them, especially since he didn't seem that old.

"You look like you're carrying everything you own." Josten moved closer to the horses. "Are you leaving?"

"Not leaving, exactly, just moving camp." She took a deep breath. It was now or never. "Do you have any places you'd recommend I settle for the duration of this event?"

He raised his eyebrows. "Was there something wrong with your previous camp?"

She nodded slowly, debating how much she should tell him. "Yeah. The biggest problem with it was it was full of men."

He gaped at her. "Full of men? Aren't they your people?"

She scowled. "No, they're not *my people*. They're just men, and I was coerced to come with them. Plus, they're not very good men."

Josten snorted. "I could've told you that just from outward observations."

She barked an unhappy laugh. "Yeah, me too. But last night made it very clear so I thought I'd move my camp closer to the Tombs. It would both be easier to do my job watching the horses and be safer."

"Safer? Camping *closer* to the Tombs?" Josten's jaw dropped. Then he narrowed his eyes. "With the Goblins and Orcs who live inside?"

She nodded. "I'd rather be among them than the men who raid their homes." She tilted her head. "Is that a problem?"

"Most humans hate being here." He waved at the cave entrance behind him.

"You live around here, don't you?" She gestured to the forest around them. "Surely you know a good place where I can camp without having to make the long trek here every day. Your place is near here, right?" She stopped and bit her lip. "I mean, would it be okay if I find a place to camp around here?"

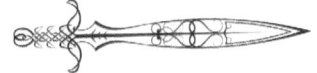

Josten's voice stuck in his throat, and he had to swallow hard a few times to unlock it. How could he tell her he 'lived' in the

Dreadstone Tombs? That she was only interacting with a ghost who normally frightened off the humans who dared enter.

It took several moments for his brain to kick back in and process the information. Allira had packed her things to find a new place to camp *closer* to him.

Closer to the Tombs, *not to me, specifically. And for safety reasons.*

Something was off about that, and uneasy anger rose at the thought. But his heart did a little dance with the idea that she'd be closer to him by default. Which was ridiculous because he was a ghost and she was very much alive, and there was no future for them together.

But if she's closer, I can protect her.

"Josten? Your place is close, right?"

He realized he'd been silent too long. "Uh, yeah, yeah, it's not far." *Just follow the invaders through the gate and you're there.*

"So, are you okay with me camping in these woods? I promise to live quietly for as long as the idiots try to raid the Tombs. I'm really just a glorified stablehand for this event, but I'd rather just have my own camp."

He frowned. "Why? I'd imagine you'd rather be with your own...people."

She scowled and shook her head. "They aren't my people. Yeah, we're all human, but they're male glory hounds. There's this constant one-upmanship going on that makes it unpleasant to be around them, and they don't see me as anything other than a camp director, or worse."

"Worse?" Josten narrowed his eyes. "What does that mean?"

Allira bit her lip and looked at the horses as if gathering her thoughts. "Being closer to where I watch the horses isn't the only reason I'd like my own camp." Her mouth flattened. "Someone tried to get into my tent last night. I'm sure if you asked him, he'd say he was drunk and mistook my tent for his own, but I have my doubts. Thank the gods I have a fair measure of battle-readiness."

Josten's hands tightened into fists, and inordinate fury rose in his chest. He wasn't a saint by any stretch of the imagination, but even at his most randy, he'd never forced a woman for sex. The idea was repugnant, and it made him want to return to the Tombs and hunt down the invaders on principle. But that wouldn't help Allira so he forced his attention back to the situation at hand.

"I do know a place that is secluded and protected, but close enough to be within walking distance for your horse-minding duties." He willed his hands to unclench. "Do you want to set up camp now?"

She nodded. "Yeah, the sooner the better. That way I know I have a safe place to go once the men come back for their mounts. Does it have enough room for my warhorse stable?"

"Uh, you'd have to set up another picket line, but it should do well enough. Why?"

"Because more than likely there will be fewer and fewer men coming out of the Tombs and I'll have to do something with their horses."

He ran his gaze over the horses waiting in the shade. "There are some good-looking mounts here. Although I think you have the two best ones already."

She grinned. "Flatterer. Come on. Show me this secluded spot so I can get the tack off them."

She took the reins of her mount and the packhorse, and nodded for him to lead the way. Josten moved off to the west of the gate, still considering her choice to be close to the Tombs. It stretched the imagination that she felt safer at the place known for death than she did with the other invaders.

Either the Tombs are losing their touch as a place of fear and dread, or the invaders are far worse.

He didn't like to think of the humans who came to the Dreadstone Tombs as being dangerous to their own people, but he wasn't much surprised. Anyone who signed up to raid the Tombs each year cared little for anything other than adventure, killing, and treasure. It didn't matter that the treasure they sought could have been given to them by the Goblins and Orcs if the humans just asked. The dwellers of the Dreadstone Caves used it as decoration for their homes, its only value in aesthetics. But the humans only saw the dwellers as monsters guarding the treasure they wanted, and they'd take it using deadly force.

Except for Allira. She apparently neither wanted the treasure nor to enter the Tombs. And she cared what the Goblins and Orcs thought of humans invading their homes.

Josten kept puzzling over her differences from other humans. She truly was a warrior—she'd proved it by the familiar patterns she'd practiced with her sword. He bit back chagrin. He hadn't entirely believed her when she'd claimed to be a fighter. She wasn't like most of the women he'd met back in his living days, but he admitted he'd seen most of them as either servants or pleasure companions.

As much as he'd like to take his pleasure with Allira, it was unlikely she'd allow it. She wasn't here to be the camp companion, and she proved she could defend herself if need-be.

Besides, it's impossible since I'm a fucking ghost.

Yeah, that was the biggest draw-back and mood-killer.

"It's really quiet out here. I never noticed near our camp—mostly because the men keep boasting about all the shit they claimed to have done. But it's nice to be able to hear the wind and birds in the trees." Allira shot him a smile.

Josten nodded. "Since the humans left the area, this place has been very calm. The denizens of the caves have found a balance with the wildlife and flora around the Dreadstone Mountains."

He led Allira down a trail that wound its way between the trees until it opened up to a small clearing against the rising walls of the Dreadstone Mountains. The space formed a natural alcove, albeit a large one, with a stream cascading down the far side in a series of short waterfalls. Tall grasses covered most of the space before the forest took over again, but there were two trees closer to the wall that made a perfect space for a tent or make-shift shelter.

"Oh, wow. I would've never known this place was here." Allira's voice held wonder as she stepped into the clearing. She glanced back at the trail they'd followed. "It's, what, about a hundred meters away from the gate?"

Josten nodded. "Yeah, a little less. Very few know about it. No one comes here so you should be safe, at least from the humans."

"Do the Goblins and Orcs come here?" She swung her gear off the packhorse and deposited it between the two trees near the wall.

He shook his head. "They feel too exposed out here, and the light is too bright for them. They prefer darker places. It's why they live in the caves."

She glanced around, looking for something. "This isn't your clearing, is it?"

"N-no, I live a bit farther away. Why?"

She shrugged. "I figured since you're the only one who comes here, it would be close to your place."

"Oh, no. I just like to come to this clearing from time to time. The stream adds background noise when I'm trying to clear my thoughts."

To be completely honest, he'd forgotten about the clearing until she'd asked for a place to stay. He hadn't visited in a while as he sank deeper into the bleak disappointment of his endless non-life.

"How do you know so much about the folks living in the Tombs?"

He shrugged. "I've been here a long time, and I started to notice patterns."

She nodded and removed the tack from her riding horse. "Will the horses be safe here if I tether them? The people in the Tombs won't see them as prey animals?"

"No, they have their own livestock and gardens inside."

"What?" Allira straightened. "Seriously?"

"Yup. They've figured out how to get the sunlight down into the darkest areas so they can grow crops without having to expose themselves to the surface."

"Now that I would like to see. It sounds pretty ingenious."

"Oh, it is. They've made huge improvements to the caves and can live pretty comfortably all year long. They even bring in fresh water so they don't have to drink cooled mineral water." Josten wished he could help her set up camp, but outside the caves he could only keep his form opaque. She'd fall right through him if she tripped, so he kept out of her way. "The hot springs keep that section of the caves warmer and are used for healing and bathing."

"Wow, I'm learning more than I ever expected from this adventure." She glanced up at the sun before she unpacked her tent and laid it out for set up. "As long as I'm safe here and the Goblins and Orcs and whatever else lives in the Tombs know I'm not a threat, this will suit me just fine."

He tried to help by creating rope tethers for the two horses so they could graze while she guarded the knights' horses back at the gate. He couldn't manipulate much, but the ropes were easy to tie around the bases of a couple of saplings with enough length for the animals to find feed.

By the time he'd finished, Allira had set up her tent and tossed her gear inside out of the weather. She retrieved halters for the two horses and attached them to the ropes he'd tied to the trees.

"There, I think that's good enough. I'll make a fire pit tonight when the knights are done for the day. Although, if I get more horses, I'm going to need to make some sort of corral to keep them."

Josten tapped his chin. "That might be a good idea. Then they'd have the run of the meadow and you wouldn't have to worry about them tangling in the ropes."

"Let's not get ahead of ourselves. There are still plenty of idiots who think they can find the treasure in the Tombs. Someone might get lucky and end this farce early."

She dug through her packs and pulled out a leather-bound journal and a pencil as well as some rations to snack on while she attended the horses. She stuffed everything into a small day-pack and slung it over her shoulder.

"Okay, I'm ready to go back to the gate."

Josten grunted but didn't say anything else as they headed back to the place where the knights had left their horses. The men who went into the Tombs wouldn't find the treasure they sought. That wasn't how the Dreadstone Curse worked.

He should know. The curse came about because of him.

Chapter Five

Allira let her breath out as they emerged from the trees to find all the horses exactly how she'd left them before setting up her own camp. That was on top of the relief of not having to ride back to the viper's den of men who saw her as a fuck toy. Having a camp away from them was the best solution.

She left her sword back at the new camp as well. While it was a formidable weapon, she preferred to have the ability to move quickly without the weight. Her dagger would be enough since she wasn't storming the Dreadstone Tombs.

Yeah, I don't need the treasure or the curse that comes with it.

While not superstitious, the few knights who came back from the Festival of the Relic were damaged beyond repair, and most didn't return at all, giving credence to the Dreadstone Curse. Whether it was true magic or just enough belief by the people, either way, the curse had power and Allira respected it enough to stay away.

Which begged the question: Why was Josten living near the Tombs?

"Josten, do you know about the Dreadstone Curse?" She settled in her usual spot near the picket line and pulled out the journal.

Josten started as if she'd goosed him. "The Dreadstone Curse? Why do you ask?"

Did he look guilty?

She shrugged. "I was just thinking that anyone who lives as close to the Tombs as you do would know about the curse that's said to cover the treasure."

He nodded. "Yes, I know about it."

"Is it real magic? Or just a very powerful belief?"

He sat silent for a long time and seemed to fade into the shade of the trees, as if he wasn't solid. A chill ghosted down her spine, and she shivered despite the mild temperature of the day.

Eventually, he shrugged. "One begets the other, I reckon."

She frowned. "What do you mean?"

He tilted his head. "Magic is just energy manipulation. Some folks are naturally adept at it, and can make astounding things happen. That's all a curse is—an astounding thing that's brought into being by the will of someone adept at energy control. And then, enough people see the results of that energy control and the curse gains power through their belief."

Allira let his explanation bounce around her thoughts. "So, you believe in the curse?"

He nodded. "Hard not to when I see fewer and fewer men come out of the Tombs each day."

"That's a very good point." She snorted. "Another reason I'm more than happy watching the horses."

"You don't have to simply watch horses."

She smirked. "Oh, I know. I could read, if I had a book with me. Or I could shadow-spar as I was doing earlier. And I have my journal. Er, Danville's empty journal." She grimaced, hoping Josten wouldn't blame her for picking over Danville's things.

I'm no better than the others in that. Hell, I even took his horse.

"Or you could come with me to gather local herbs for the Goblin medicine woman I know."

"What?" Allira shook herself out of her thoughts. "You collect herbs for the Goblins?"

"Only on rare occasions when I have a friendly helper with me." He shot her a sly smirk.

"Oh, is *that* all I am? A friendly helper?" She glared but her grin ruined the effect as she shoved her journal back into her day pack.

His smirk widened. "Of course. Or you could just sit here watching the horses napping in the shade. Your choice."

She rolled her eyes. "Fine. What kinds of herbs are you looking for? Medicinal?"

He nodded. "For the most part. I find what I can for the Goblins because they don't like coming out of the Tombs if they can help it. And especially not when the invaders are here."

Allira slung her pack over her shoulders. "Yeah, I can imagine they don't want to leave their homes undefended. But you also said they have their own gardens in the Tombs. Can't they grow their own herbs, as well?"

"They can, but some things don't do well in controlled environments." He headed away from the horses in the opposite direction of her camp. "Also, why wait for something to grow when you can harvest it already grown?"

"Fair. I just can't go far from the horses. I need to stay close enough to keep an eye on them."

Josten nodded. "We won't go beyond the edge of the clearing." He pointed to the tree line and the shrubs growing beneath them.

She glanced at the horses to check that all was calm, but nodded. "All right."

He led her into the trees opposite the trail to her camp and they moved about, scrutinizing the shrubbery and collecting various plants in handfuls. He pointed out the Burn Bane meant to help with both blisters and burns; the cream succulents that could be boiled and distilled down into skin protectants. And the 'poop root,' a fibrous root from the satin flower that helped with constipation.

Allira recognized some of the plants from those her grandmothers often collected and distilled into useful items for healing and health, but some were new and she took leaf samples to press between the pages of the journal for later description.

Two other herbs seemed particularly useful—'pain bane' which could be used for pain relief on broken bones and open wounds, and 'spark bark' which was a restorative that gave quick and plentiful energy, especially when a being needed to stay awake for various reasons. It could be dried and chewed, or boiled and drunk to get the effects of the herb.

"Gotta love the names Goblins and Orcs give their medicinals." Allira smirked as she collected some spark bark off the trees.

"They might not be very original, but when you're suffering from something, why bother with fancy names when 'poop root' does the trick?"

She laughed. "Very good point."

They passed the afternoon making small piles of items. He pointed out most of the herbs, and she gathered them, but after a while she realized he hadn't touched anything. After the third time where he pointed to some 'pain bane' but didn't touch it, she gathered it and paused.

"How are we going to take this back to the gate? I certainly don't have enough hands."

He waved away her concerns. "We won't. We'll leave them here to dry a bit, and I'll bring the Medicine Woman's assistants back to collect them this evening after the sun goes down."

Allira raised an eyebrow. "Are you sure they'll be safe and no animals will eat your neat piles?"

"I'm sure. They'll be fine. Now, if—"

Josten cut himself off and turned back toward the gate to the Tombs, his expression darkening. For just a moment, she thought she saw him shift into a fearsome, skeletal warrior, with glowing green eyes the same color as sunlight on emeralds. A chill ran over Allira, and she stepped back from him, her hands tightening on the herbs she still held.

"Josten?"

He growled, anger churning in the sound. "I must go."

That was all he said before he took off back toward the gate.

"Josten, wait!"

Allira dropped the herbs and hurried after him, but despite running full out, by the time she reached the horses, Josten had vanished. She glanced around, out of breath, to see where he'd gone, but he'd disappeared.

How the hell can he move that fast and quiet? He's bigger than me!

She shook her head, perplexed, as she made her way over to the horses and dropped her day pack. The animals looked rested and calm, most with their hind feet cocked in relaxation. She glanced up at the sun. It still sat high in the sky, too early for anyone to be coming out. Despite that, she had the urge to replace bridles and tighten girth straps.

What the hell just happened?

She shook her head and rubbed her arms, still affected by the chill she'd felt earlier. Her gut churned with unease and insisted she'd better hop-to, or the consequences could be dire. She groaned and moved to make sure each horse wore its bridle properly, contentedly chewing on its bit. Then she went back through and tightened each saddle to be ready for its rider.

I'm crazy to be doing this.

She almost relented and undid all her work, but another chill ran through just before a shriek shattered the peaceful afternoon, making her jump. All the horses spooked, yanking against the picket line. Some reared in panic, their eyes rolling white.

"Whoa!"

Allira grabbed the nearest horse and the line, hauling back against the animal's panicked motions. She managed to calm it down enough to get to the others so they wouldn't shear the rope apart, but it didn't matter. A roar blasted out of the gate, raising the hair on the back of her neck.

She spun around, wishing she'd brought her sword as she faced the gate. The knights came boiling out of the Tombs, their faces white as snow and their clothes covered in blood and battle scars.

"Untie the fuckin' horses, Maplestaff!" Swindell charged straight at her.

She almost told him to fuck off, but decided fast action was the better part of valor. She tried to unloop the reins from the picket line as the men scrambled toward their mounts.

Swearing and snarling ensued when they couldn't get their horses free as quick as they liked. She did the best she could to help, but once the animals were untangled from the rope, they took off like the hounds of hell nipped at their heels, making the men run after them. She scrubbed her face with her hands and tried to catch her breath.

Holy shit!

A new sound had her spinning around to face the gate. Goblins and Orcs flooded out of the Tombs, their faces pulled into monstrous snarls as they shrieked at the retreating men. They threw sticks and cobbles after them, and Allira found herself grateful she stood out of the way of their rising ire.

Then they turned their attention to her.

Oh shit.

Josten hadn't had a chance to talk to the Goblins and Orcs about her staying nearby, and they definitely looked at her like she was an additional threat. Fortunately, she *didn't* have her sword, and she raised her hands in the universal sign of surrender, hoping it would be enough. The Orcs bellowed, but the Goblins sniffed the air as if trying to determine her status by scent alone.

Should I wave or just stand here?

Allira swallowed hard and tried to get her mind in gear. If they decided she was a threat now, they'd never let her stay near the Tombs. Hell, she wouldn't live long enough to make it to her camp. She shifted closer to one of the three remaining horses, planning to use one to make her escape.

Wait, three?

She glanced quickly at the animals standing at sharp attention and realized the knights had lost three more of their brethren—Altarman, Tinsley, and Dinsmoore. Damn. She was glad she'd left the camp. The men would be squabbling over the dead knights' gear, but the horses were hers if she wanted them.

If I survive to keep them.

A roar sounded from the Goblins and Orcs, and random pieces of armor flew into the clearing in front of the gates. Bloodied and dented from battle, they fell heavily with loud thuds. It took her a few moments to realize they were full of body parts, still dripping with bodily fluids. She swallowed against her rising gorge and braced herself for movement—either onto a mount or into defensive moves.

One of the Goblins saw her and sneered, stalking ahead of the others a few steps. Allira's hand tightened on the horse's reins, and she took a deep breath.

"Begone!"

The single word thundered across the space between them, making Allira jump.

To be honest, she'd had no idea Goblins could speak, much less speak in languages she could understand. Additionally, she didn't know what to say in response. She couldn't tell them she wasn't with the men—obviously she was there with their horses and she was human. But if she told the Goblins and Orcs she had no intention of entering their home, they'd laugh with derision and probably attack.

So much for making a good impression as a friendly and harmless neighbor.

"Take your refuse and go!"

The Goblin gestured to the body parts littering the clearing.

Well, this is awkward.

"I, uh, yes, of course." She made sure all the horses were tied together before she swung up into the saddle of the dappled gray which she thought had belonged to Dinsmoore. She turned the horses to ride toward her new camp when the crowd snarled.

"Oi! Where are you going? Clean up this mess!"

She paused and glanced over her shoulder at the waiting Goblins and Orcs. "You told me to take my things and go. The only things that belong to me are the horses. I certainly didn't make a mess of your clearing."

The Goblin gaped at her as if she'd grown another head and possibly a tail. "They're *your* men."

Oh, that would have my grandmothers cackling.

She dropped her gaze to the body bits littering the ground. What was left of the knights couldn't even be termed as human.

"They're not my men. I was conscripted into watching their horses for them and collecting said horses when they failed to return." She glanced at the body parts again. "Those aren't mine." She almost rode away, but tried a peace offering. "But if you'd like help parsing out armor and weapons, I can return after I've seen to the animals."

There was a moment of silence before the crowd of Orcs and Goblins burst out laughing.

"You wish to help us, human?"

She shrugged, though her heart pounded in her chest. "Sure, I'd be happy to help. I'm sure some of the things they were carrying would be useful and fit my hands better than those of your warriors. As for the body parts, I have no need of them. Perhaps you have use for the meat?"

Another silence ensued as the Goblins and Orcs exchanged perplexed looks.

"Human meat tastes like shit." One of the Orcs spat on the ground.

"I don't doubt that for a minute. I've seen what they eat." She snorted. "Maybe you could feed it to your carnivore pets. Let me take care of these horses and I shall return to go through the remains."

"Fine." The speaking Goblin snarled. "Just stay out of our caves."

"Of course." She nodded and rode away before they changed their minds, her shoulder blades itching with their hard gazes on her back.

Chapter Six

J osten scowled as he took in the bloody and broken bodies of the Goblins left to rot outside the entrance to the gardens in the deepest part of the Tombs. Overpowered by the greedy men intent on finding treasure, they'd died defending their farm. But in their haste to find gold, the men had destroyed some of the necessary crops for the coming winter, and the Goblins had come to drive them out.

One of the Goblins killed was the local chieftain who oversaw the annual planting and delivery of nutrients to keep the soil fertile. She'd been a child when Josten left his mortal remains on the throne, and he'd watched her grow into a fine leader and a talented horticulturalist. Now she lay dead on the polished paving stones she'd laid down as a path.

Fury and grief rolled through him in alternating waves, and he wished he could punish the barbaric men who'd defiled this sacred place all for the promise of gold. In the end, he hadn't needed to punish them. The Goblins and Orcs had done it for him, chasing the remaining living men out after killing three of them. They hacked the bodies up and threw them out of the Tombs to litter the clearing in front of the gate as a warning.

A warning the stupid fools will ignore because treasure.

Josten sat to the side as the dead were cleaned and wrapped in course spun cloth. Flowers from the Death's Heart Orchid were stitched into the wrapping over the chest of each body. The bodies were carried deeper into the caverns where the river of molten rock flowed, keeping the caves warm in the winter and heating the hot springs and bathing pools.

After singing the Journey Song, each body was cast into the flowing rock, returning them to the earth from which all were born. With the chieftain, they cleaned and wrapped her body before carrying it past all the different clan families so they could pay their respects before she was taken out to the fields on the east side of the Tombs and buried in the ground to restore the nutrients to the land. Josten stayed within the shadow of the Tombs, but his heart wept for the chieftain's loss.

This is all my fault. It's my curse that causes this annual tragedy.

Anger and frustration stirred, and he thought of Allira. She'd come with the men who raided and killed on a yearly basis, and he wanted to blame her. Yet, he couldn't find it in himself to hate her. She'd never shown any interest in going into the Tombs after the reputed treasure, and she'd made it clear she'd only come because she'd been conscripted. Watching the horses during the day gave her something to do.

However, the Goblins and Orcs wouldn't see her that way.

Oh dreck! Allira!

Josten bolted back into the caves, phasing through walls, and headed for the front gate. He passed the others heading back to their chores without a word, hoping the warriors wouldn't attack Allira because she was human. But they'd seen what humans did to their homes and Allira would be marked as one of the invaders.

Fear curdled his gut for the first time in over a century as he fled toward the gate. There was no one in the entrance, not even the pieces of the dead knights who'd entered. Where had they gone?

Josten reached the clearing and stopped short, his jaw dropping.

The horses were gone, and the Orcs and Goblins still milled about. But Allira moved among them as they picked over the torn and broken bodies of the dead knights. And they seemed to ask *her* what she thought about each piece.

She would study the bit left over and pull off chain mail to lay it on the ground before handing over the rest to the nearest Orc. They'd confer a moment before either tossing the bit into a pile of others or taking extra time to remove more from it. Once the useable gear was removed, a Goblin collected it to start the cleaning process while the flesh was added to the pile.

Josten gaped as a female Goblin came up to Allira and held up pieces of the chain mail. Allira nodded and pointed to where things could be linked back together. They spoke a few more moments before another Goblin, male this time, brought another body part.

Josten moved among the Orcs gathering up the pieces to haul away for burning and closed in on Allira as she peeled the ruined tabbard off a knight's headless torso. She tossed it aside, nearly hitting him.

"Oh glory! Sorry, Josten. I didn't see you there."

"Evidently. What are you doing?"

Allira shot him a raised eyebrow. "Helping the Cawrhi Clan find useful items from the invaders. Gundri, this might work as straps to help carry water for your hanging planters." She held up one of the leather belts that the dead man had wrapped around his waist twice.

Gundri, a female Goblin who fought as fiercely as the male Orcs, nodded as she took the plain leather belt. "Much thanks, Allira-dri."

"Allira-dri?" Josten raised both his eyebrows. "They're calling you by an honorific now?"

"Is that what it is? I thought it was something like 'miss' or 'sir,' just a generic term of respect." She shrugged before wiping her forehead with her arm.

"Okay, what's going on? How...? I was sure they'd attack you." He gestured to the teams of Orcs and Goblins working to clean up the dead and separating out gear into useable and trash piles.

She nodded. "They almost did, but then I offered to help them separate the gear from the bodies. I think they thought I was kidding. But once I took the horses back to my camp, I returned like I promised." She shrugged as if it wasn't a big deal. "I've been helping them clean up the mess by sorting out the useful items from the dross. They seem to appreciate it."

"They...do." It wasn't really a question, as it was obvious. "Why?"

"I don't actually know. I guess I don't smell like the other humans. Or maybe my smell had never entered the Tombs." She shrugged again. "Either way, I think they're okay that I'm a neighbor like you, as long as I stay out."

She gave him a smile as another Orc brought a large pair of legs to her.

"Excuse me, Josten."

She helped the Orc, Tral, pull the boots off. One would have to be stitched back up the shank, but the rest was in decent condition despite the stain of blood. Tral inclined his head to Josten before he carried the boots away.

For a while, Josten simply watched the Goblins and Orcs work with Allira, his mind in a strange state of amazement. Dreadstone Caves dwellers working *with* a human? It didn't seem possible. Especially after the days the denizens of the Tombs had experienced threat and death from the invading humans. But the Cawrhi Clan worked side by side with Allira until the whole clearing was clean and the useful items slowly carried back into the caves for distribution.

"Thank you, Allira-dri!" Tral waved as he heaved a large pile of plate armor onto his shoulders.

Allira nodded and waved to the warriors as they disappeared through the gate. She wiped her forehead again before moving to a small pile of items on the ground near where the horses had stood.

Most of it was smaller weapons like daggers and knives, but there was one sword with the tip broken off.

"Why are you keeping that?" Josten pointed to the broken sword.

"Oh, hey. You're still here." She gave him a tired smile. "I thought it would make a lovely boundary marker. See the opalite crystal pommel? It would catch the light beautifully in the sun." She dipped the pommel into the westering sunlight. "I figure I'd drive it into the ground tip first and let it mark the entrance to my camp. There wasn't another one as nice so I'll have to wait to see who drops what."

He couldn't help it. He laughed. "You're going to use the knights' dropped, broken weapons as decoration of your camp?"

"Sure, why not?" She grinned as she carefully picked up the items one by one. "They're not using them. I got the idea from Gundri. She said they often use the jewels as light-catching decorations in their homes. I thought it a good use of broken junk."

Josten coughed in amused disbelief. "I guess that's one way to think of it."

"Hey, thanks for coming to check on me. I appreciate it." She gave him a nod as she picked her way toward her camp. "When you get a chance, you might want to tell the Cawrhi Clan I'll be watching the horses and live nearby. I don't want them surprised to see me again."

"Why didn't you tell them when they were here?"

She shrugged one shoulder. "We didn't get to that conversation. There was too much cleanup to do, and they needed to get back into their homes where they felt safe."

"Are you headed back to your camp?" He realized it was a dumb question the moment he said it, but it was already out there.

She grinned. "Yup. I'm gonna decorate with what I have before the sun goes down completely and make some supper. You're welcome to join me if you have nothing else to do."

It took him a few moments to realize she'd invited him for the evening meal.

"I'd like to, but I do have something to do, first." He gave her a rueful smile. "One of the Goblin chieftains was killed today, and I need to pay my last respects. I was at the ceremony when I realized the warriors were out here with you."

"Oh no." Allira's expression crumpled into sorrow. "I'm so sorry." She shook her head. "This tradition of raiding the Tombs is horseshit. Please offer my condolences for their loss."

He was touched by her sentiment. "I will. And I'll see you after."

She turned to continue on her way, and Josten found himself tempted to follow her to camp. The sun painted a golden halo around her as she walked away, and he couldn't help but enjoy the sway of her hips. To his surprise, his body reacted, hardening his cock at the vision.

What would she look like spread out before him? What would she taste like if he could feast on her womanly parts?

What does it matter since I'm a ghost?

Crushing disappointment hit his chest and he forced his feet back toward the Tombs, his heart heavy, and not just because of the chieftain's loss. He was stuck in his twilight existence because of his greed and fear, and nothing would change that. He couldn't even properly die. He nodded to a few of the Orcs he passed in the caves as he continued to the eastern fields. There were torches burning around the grave, but all of the mourners had gone. He was glad of the solitude as he settled himself deeper into the shadows beyond the torchlight and closed his eyes.

The grave site glimmered with energy and light despite the one buried within having gone. Death energy was different than life energy, but no less powerful. It was why some sorcerers practiced with death magic. He himself was the result of death magic and greed, two powerful forces holding him in the Dreadstone Tombs.

And I signed up for this tour voluntarily.

But for the last few decades, he'd wished for an ending to his bleak existence, praying for the release that was true death. He'd grown weary of being the Dreadstone King, the one to haunt, maim, kill, and terrify the humans who came to raid the Tombs of "his" treasure. Jaded and resigned, he'd drifted through the seasons until they all blurred together.

Until Allira came.

Allira, who showed him the value of his existence, through caring about others and respecting the boundaries of the residents of the caves. She'd reminded him there were things more valuable than trinkets, gold, and power.

Josten let his thoughts tumble over themselves as he watched the strains of energy flit from the grave into the surrounding field. The chieftain's body was already breaking down, releasing life and nutrients back into the soil. No one else could see it, but he remembered it from all the times he'd killed someone.

The more rotten their spirit, the more quickly the life energy drained into the ground and slithered away to be resorbed. Most of the men who came to the Tombs were like that, though a few had been brighter lights, there for reasons other than gold and power. Their energy swirled around the Tombs for a few hours before finally settling into the molten river and returning to the source.

Would his energy be like that when he was finally released? Or would it slink away into the earth to be dissipated and forgotten? Josten snorted. He couldn't claim his spirit didn't have the same rot that drove the raiding men. He'd killed enough people in his time. But he'd also seen the Goblins and Orcs build up their homes and civilization, shared a few ideas to help them improve the caves, and protected them as much as possible from the raiders when they harmed the village, especially in recent years.

Josten shook his head and snorted. There wasn't much hope of change for him, but at least he had something more to do than just drift through the caves on his own. Allira was here for as long as the men kept raiding, and that would have to be enough.

But it won't last forever, and she'll be gone again, soon.

The thought settled into his gut with the weight of cold iron. He was bound to the Tombs, and it had become his own. The curse held him there and wasn't likely to be broken, especially by the men currently raiding. The crushing disappointment returned and bleak despair settled in behind it. It took Josten a long time to find the energy to get up and leave the grave site.

Chapter Seven

Allira started a fire before she did anything else so the coals would be ready for cooking by the time she got all the horses situated. She'd started out with two, and now she had five, with all their tack.

"I'm going to need a wagon to haul all this stuff back to Capstone Creek at this rate." She patted Javalina. "At least you won't have to haul it all alone. Now we have a whole team."

She shook her head and turned her attention to decorating her camp. She eyed her space and decided she needed a little perimeter fence. Broken swords and shields weren't usual for camp demarcation, but when she'd set up the few she had, she was pleased with the result. It reminded her of a little yard in front of a cottage.

Not that she had a cottage, but she did have a lovely little yard.

She filled up her canteen and those collected from the dead knights' gear, and settled down to make a small pot of stew. The evening deepened, and she listened to the horses and the wind in the trees around her camp, letting her tension flow away. This was the way camp was supposed to be. Quiet, reflective, and safe. She didn't regret leaving the knights' camp at all.

No more being hyper-vigilant, always looking over my shoulder.

Not that she was safe from all predators, but at least she didn't have to worry about human threats this close to the Tombs.

The sky to the west turned molten orange and gold before tapering into indigo with a brilliant spattering of sparkling stars. She glanced around her camp and wondered what it would be like to call the meadow and the space between the trees permanently home. She'd have to start a garden, and maybe get chickens for meat and eggs. Of course, this close to a forest meant there'd be predators like foxes and bobcats who'd enjoy her chickens for the same reason. Which meant she'd need to build a coop for them.

Allira laughed and shook her head. "Look at me, already planning a mini-farm, when I can just go home to a larger one."

"Do you always talk to yourself aloud?"

Allira jumped as Josten appeared just beyond the fire, and she forced herself to loosen her hand around her kitchen knife.

"Good glory, you scared the daylights outta me." She shook her head and settled back down.

"Sorry." He grimaced and raised his hands. "I didn't mean to startle you. You were expecting me, right?"

She let her breath out slowly. "Yeah, right, I was. Come and sit down. I have some stew cooking if you haven't eaten."

He gave her an apologetic smile as he settled on one of the stones she'd moved close to the fire. "I grabbed something at home. I've brought something for you, though."

He held out a thick rectangular item wrapped in oilcloth, and she rose to take it.

"What's this?"

"Open it. I thought you'd like it."

Curiosity burned in her chest as she carefully unwrapped the hard bundle. In the light of the fire, she pulled out a leather-bound book covered in dust despite the oilcloth. She tilted the binding to read the title.

"The Lesser-Known Cases of Torsha the Bold." Allira raised her eyebrows. "Is this a book of Torsha Mallesdautr, the famous detective from Calistonia?"

"One and the same." He nodded with a faint smile. "You've heard of Torsha?"

"Are you kidding? My Mima Hestia used to tell me tales of Torsha's bravery and smarts every night before I went to bed. And Nanna Esme actually knew Torsha back when they were girls in the same village." Allira grinned as she hugged the book. "We didn't have a copy of the Lesser-Known Cases, but I've always wanted to read it."

Josten raised his eyebrows. "Your grandmother knew Torsha?"

"Yeah, she said the woman was the sharpest person she'd ever met. I so wanted to be like Torsha, a renowned detective who could see patterns where others couldn't, but my talents didn't run in that direction." She sighed and shot him a rueful smile. "I was better at fighting and tracking than I was at seeing hidden clues and mysteries." She held up the book. "Thank you for this. It'll make my days go by a little faster while watching the horses."

"Speaking of horses." He nodded to the variety of faces on the picket line just beyond the fire. "It seems like your herd is growing."

She glanced over her shoulder at Javalina and crew. "Yup. I acquired three more today. They used to belong to the owners of the various pieces we cleaned up this evening." She set the book aside away from the fire, before checking on the stew. "Are you sure I can't tempt you with a bowl? It's almost done and it's pretty good, if I do say so myself."

He shook his head. "I'm sure. Tell me what you're planning to do when the knights come back tomorrow."

She shrugged. "Half of them are dead or injured. By my count, there should only be six left still able to raid the Tombs. Five are dead, one is badly injured, and I'm the seventh who won't go in unless invited. That leaves Marcus Swindell, Abel Kettering, Sir Milford Argyle, and three others whose names I don't remember well. They usually go in six at a time, but we'll see how tomorrow goes."

Josten nodded then glanced around her camp. "This has turned out to be rather homey. And the sword and shields do make a nice decorative fence."

Allira ducked her head and shrugged with one shoulder. "Thanks. My temporary home away from home."

"I heard you mentioning something about a garden?"

She licked her lips. "Yeah, I was thinking if I actually stayed here long-term, I'd need a garden and a chicken coop so I could get fresh eggs. But it's kinda a silly dream because this is just temporary. But I really like it here."

"Do you?" His gaze sharpened. Was that hope on his face?

"Yeah. It's quiet, and no one bothers me. There's shelter from the wind and weather, mostly, and there's fresh water. And now I have this little yard where I can sit and enjoy the fire without worrying someone will sneak up on me." She shot him a dry smirk. "Except for you, of course."

He had the grace to look chagrinned. "Sorry, again. I didn't mean to do that. Do you expect the other men to sneak up on you?"

She shook her head slowly. "I don't think so. Most of them don't know where I've gone and unless they're looking, wouldn't come this direction. Still, I'll keep an ear out in case anyone tries something."

His jaw tightened and his lips flattened, but he nodded. "Those knights don't strike me as honorable."

She snorted. "Anyone who raids other people's homes for treasure isn't honorable by any stretch of the imagination."

"I can't argue that." He scrubbed his face with his hands. "But wouldn't it be safer with them to keep watch?"

She raised an eyebrow. "Keep watch for whom? They're the ones who are the threat."

He blinked. "You make a very good point. Personally, I'm glad you've distanced yourself from them."

"Yeah? Me too." She blew her breath out, checking on her stew. "I'll sleep better at night, and bonus, I get to be closer to the Tombs."

He tilted his head, his gaze intent again. "How is that a bonus?"

Allira suddenly found it hard to speak and yet, she was desperate to tell him how she felt as the heat rose to her cheeks. "I, uh. Well, I kinda hoped I could hang out with you more." She dropped her gaze to the stew. "You're better company, I feel like I can trust you not to hurt me, and... I like you."

She *did* like him. Weirdly, spending time with Josten the last few days had made the whole conscription seem not so bad. Of course, she wasn't sure what would happen when she returned to her grandmothers' place without the treasure or the other 'heroes.' She was guaranteed to live, but she didn't want to win the hand of the princess or become the Dreadstone King.

And I definitely don't want the Relic.

"I like you, too, Allira. More than I expected of the knights who come to raid the Tombs."

She grimaced. "Fortunately, I'm not one of them."

He inclined his head. "No, you are not. A fact I'm very grateful for. I definitely wouldn't share my books with them."

"Which means they're missing out. Thank you again for this book." She held it up, enjoying the embossed cover. "I'll truly enjoy reading it."

"Perhaps you could read it to me when we visit."

She raised her eyebrows as a thrill ran through her. "Haven't you read it already?"

He shook his head and rubbed the back of his neck. "I haven't. I was a little busy when I received my copy, and it fell by the wayside."

"I know how that is. My TBR pile is beyond reckoning." She nodded, thinking of all the books she had at home waiting for her. Not that she'd be getting back to them anytime soon. Or sooner than she expected if the knights kept dying as fast as they were.

"Do you read a lot?" He crossed his feet at the ankles, appearing to settle in for a while.

She grimaced as she stirred the stew. "Not as much as I'd like to. I used to read all the time as a child when I was done with my farm chores, but now I just seem to collect books without reading them." She waved her hand at the one he'd brought.

He laughed. "That's the truth of it for me. So many books, so little time."

"Why is that a truism?" She frowned. "We need to change that. Like, it should be, 'All the books, all the time' or something similar. Of course, on a farm, there are always chores so reading becomes a luxury."

"Didn't you just say you were thinking of making a little farm here?"

She groaned. "Yeah, that's what I was saying. I mean, if I want eggs, I'll need chickens, and for chickens, I'll need a coop to keep them safe from the predators. And I'll need a garden to grow vegetables..." She gestured helplessly at the world beyond the fire.

"Does that mean you're thinking of staying?"

Allira took her time in answering as she stirred the stew, letting the question bounce around inside her. *Was* she thinking of staying? Would it suit her? It was too early to make a final decision on permanence. Hell, she'd just set up her own camp that morning and she didn't have a house, a corral, or a garden yet. All she had were broken and discarded weaponry as yard decorations.

But she'd been mulling over what she'd do when she returned to Capstone Creek. Would she continue being a knight-for-hire? Get long-trip security work? Join a mercenary group like Josten once did? Or would she just go back to being a farmer with her grandmothers?

The more she thought about it, the more tired she got. Always fighting just to get paid—literally. And all that waited for her if she quit was unending farm chores.

I guess the question comes down to which sucks less.

Unless she stayed near the Tombs where it was quiet, but there weren't any humans. Not necessarily a bad thing given how awful the humans she'd been around were to others. Hell, the Goblins and Orcs had been more friendly and respectful. They made good neighbors.

She finally sat back and scrubbed her face with her hands. "I don't know. I mean, can I stay here? Who are the people who maintain this land? Am I an interloper? Plus, what would I do? I could live quietly here, but I'd need some sort of income and if I want to farm, I might as well go home." She groaned and dropped her head back. "There isn't an easy solution."

"Slow down, I can't keep up with your thoughts." He laughed, but it held no derisiveness. "The people who occupy this land are the denizens of the Tombs, but as I've said, they don't like to come outside much. I'm sure if you talked to the Council of Elders, you could advocate for the right to stay."

"I'm human. What would make them think I'm worth having as a neighbor?"

"Two things come to mind. First, some of them have met you and know you're not interested in raiding their homes—that right there makes you a damn good neighbor." He grinned as she rolled her eyes. "But second, you could always offer something in trade."

She couldn't help the disbelieving laugh. "Have you seen my camp? I'm decorating with discarded and broken gear as lawn ornaments. What do I have to trade?"

"You said you were a mercenary for a while. Have you thought about security work?"

She narrowed her eyes. "What kind of security work? Right now, I'm perfectly happy not fighting when I'm not required."

Josten shrugged. "I was thinking you could be security *for* the denizens of the Tombs. A caretaker, if you will. Someone to be a deterrent for anyone seeking fame and fortune by raiding the Dreadstone Tombs. You could trade your efforts to protect and deter for their permission to make your home here. I could put in a good word for you, if you like."

She sipped the stew and determined it had cooked enough. "Why would you do that for me?"

He smirked. "To quote a woman I know, 'you're better company, I feel like I can trust you not to hurt me, and I like you.'"

She snorted, but his words filled her chest with warmth as she dished out two bowls of stew, and handed him one. For an awkward moment, he simply stared at it with something akin to horror, and she wondered if she'd stumbled across a faux pas she wasn't aware of.

"I'm sorry, I forgot you said you already ate." She retracted her hand and dumped the stew back into the pot. "But if you get hungry later, there's plenty."

"Uh, yeah, okay. Sounds good." He rubbed the back of his neck.

She set her bowl down and scrubbed her face with her hands. "Sorry, I must be more tired than I thought. You said you ate when you arrived." She shook her head as she took her own bowl and sat down. "So, you think the residents of the Tombs would be okay with me sticking around?"

He rested his hands in his lap as he considered her across the fire. "I think it could be beneficial for you both. You have skills in fighting, but any human who comes here would recognize you as a person, unlike Goblins or Orcs. They'd listen to you."

She snorted. "I'm not sure about that. Anyone coming here for treasure wouldn't be warned away by a single woman sitting around gathering herbs. They'd think I was hoarding the treasure for myself and go in to look, anyway."

"Maybe, but you'd be surprised by how many people are deterred by a confident authority telling them not to do something."

She shook her head. "Not treasure hunters." She stirred her stew with her spoon to allow it to cool as she mulled it over. "But I like Gundri and the others I met today. They seemed okay with me being around. I don't know how much help I could be at keeping the raiders at bay, but I'd do what I could if given the chance." She met Josten's gaze. "The Cawhri Clan were fine with me as long as I wasn't infringing on their space, but as a full-time neighbor?" She shook her head. "That could be another story."

Josten gave her a one-shouldered shrug. "I think you've won enough goodwill to at least be heard if you want to stay. And I'd stand up for you, too."

She tilted her head. "Who are you to these people? I realize you live around here, but you look as human as me—" She held up her hands, one holding the spoon—"Not that I'm making a judgment here. I admit you could be Fae or another species that I haven't met before. How did you come to be here?"

She spooned stew into her mouth as she waited for his answer.

Josten froze for the second time that night. When she'd offered him the stew he hadn't known what to do. While he could sometimes affect material things when he focused, he couldn't just grab anything on the fly. He'd been afraid the bowl would drop and spill stew onto the ground.

That would've been awkward.

And given his immaterial self, what could he tell Allira about how and why he was living near the Goblins and Orcs?

Oh, you know, I was the Dreadstone King when I was alive and pretty much ruled over all of the Tombs. Now I'm a ghostly guardian who helps them scare off the bastards who come to raid them every late summer.

Yeah, that would totally go over well. At least she was right about one thing: he was a species of being she hadn't met before. Ghosts didn't have a colony, village or even a union. As far as Josten knew, he was the only one—in the Tombs or otherwise.

"I've known Mectarn, the Medicine Woman, a long time. She and her clan moved in after I'd lived here a few years." *Understatement of the night.* "The people who live in the Tombs tolerate me because I was here first. Most of them were wary of me at first, but got used to me the longer they stayed."

Allira nodded. "Do you do anything for them? Or are you just a neighbor? I know you gather herbs for them, but I don't know much about what you do day-to-day. Is it a trade system like you suggested for me?"

He tilted his head back and forth. "Of sorts. I gather the herbs and things that don't grow in their gardens for them. I help protect their children when the little ones get overzealous in their pursuit of adventure, and I do what I can to scare off the invaders."

Like turn into a hideous skeleton with flaming green eyes and a matching sword.

"And with all that, you don't have time to read? I can't imagine why." Amused sarcasm wrapped around Josten like a warm blanket.

It doesn't help that I can't always turn the pages when I want to.

"Free time is in short supply, especially when it's the season of invasion." He tried to shrug it off. "Which is why, if you happen to have the interest of reading your new book aloud, I won't be disappointed."

She laughed and pointed her spoon at him. "Oh, I get it now. You just want someone to read to you, like a bedtime story."

"Hey, do you know how long it's been since someone read me a bedtime story? Decades. But since you're offering, I'll graciously take you up on it." He grinned.

She laughed again, and the melodic sound cracked the ice around his heart. Oh to hear that laugh every day. He wished he could convince her to stay, if only to spend more time with her. What little he knew about her made him want to learn more. He hoped she'd be interested in staying, and he'd do everything he could to convince her.

Even if I only get to talk to her. Ghosts couldn't touch their loved ones. He stilled. *Since when is she a loved one?*

Allira set her empty bowl aside. "Oh, you will, will you? All right, smartypants. How are we going to read when I don't have a lantern?"

"No lantern? What kind of a camp is this?" He rose in mock-indignation. "I was expecting a five-star establishment, not this mockery of luxury."

"Hey, pal, I'll have you know I have the best broken gear décor of anyone in the seven kingdoms. Good luck finding that at some hoity-toity five-star lodging." She raised her chin, though her grin ruined her acerbic words.

He barked a laugh, delighted by her banter. "The décor has its charms. But no lantern?" He clucked his tongue and shook his head.

"No one said you had to stay in my luxury-less camp. But if you find my hospitality so lacking, you could've brought a lantern along with your book. It was dark when you left your place."

He nodded ruefully, wishing he'd had the focus to carry a lantern along with the book. "Next time, I promise."

"I'll take you up on that. Tonight, we'll have to make due with the light of the fire. Give me a second."

She finished her stew and gathered up her dishes to rinse using a little water. She even rinsed his unused bowl before packing them up with her gear. Then she returned to her rock and grasped the book, opening it up to the first page.

"Ready?"

He leaned forward, his elbows on his knees, and rested his head on his woven fingers. "Ready."

She laughed at his eager expression. "The Case of the Gilded Gargoyle."

Josten snorted. "Who'd gild a gargoyle?"

"No idea. Hush, and we'll find out."

The rest of the evening was the best one he'd had in a century or more. Listening to Allira read the mystery adventure of Torsha the

Bold settled Josten's soul in ways he hadn't expected. He wasn't a restless ghost per se, but angst was his thing. He'd been alone for so long he hadn't realized he'd been lonely. But spending time with Allira, sharing in the same delight in Torsha's adventures, pushed back the discontent and loneliness for the first time ever. He didn't remember a time when he wasn't uneasy and brooding, always looking for something better, even while alive.

In life, it had been a strength. But in death—or whatever he experienced now—it was more a curse and a burden. And that drive had gotten him into the whole undead schtick.

When Allira started to yawn in the middle of her sentences, he realized she needed rest while he no longer slept. Not much downtime needed for the undead.

"Okay, I think it's time for you to get into bed before you fall into the fire." Josten rose and used just enough energy to brush Allira's shoulder. "Come on, you should get some rest. Big day tomorrow, watching horses and all that."

She snorted and closed the book, using a dried leaf as a bookmark. "Hey, it'll give me time to consider settling here permanently. If that's even an option. Again, I don't want to overstep the goodwill of the people in the Tombs."

"Perhaps tomorrow you'll be able to ask them." He guided her to her tent and watched her take off her boots. "And I'll try to remember to bring a real lantern when I come by after."

"Oh, you'll be back again tomorrow evening?"

"Hell yeah. I gotta know who killed the salamander's niece and what her murder has to do with the gilded gargoyle."

"Okay..." Allira yawned again then groaned. "I gotta bank the fire."

"Don't worry. I'll take care of it. You just get some sleep and I'll see you in the morning for your horse-watching shift."

She gave a tired laugh. "When you say it like that, it sounds like a minimum-wage job."

"I don't know. You usually get a new horse at the end of each shift."

"Heh, touché." She smiled as she closed her eyes. "Goodnight, Josten. Thanks for the book."

"You're welcome, Allira."

He watched her roll over and settle in to sleep, and his heart ached with yearning. He wished he could cuddle up with her, wrapping her in his arms, and snuggle down to sleep. Which was weird—he'd never wanted anyone before, human, Goblin, or Orc. Sure, there'd been some lovely females throughout the years, but no one ever tempted him like Allira.

Shaking his head, he made sure to bank the fire so it would be easy to rekindle in the morning, and faded away from her camp.

It was easy to rematerialize back in the Tombs—all he had to do was think of his throne and he'd be there. He simply pictured his own skeleton seated on the chair, faded rags draped over the dusty bones, and an iron, spiked crown on his bony skull, and phased.

The Dreadstone King, I presume.

What would Allira think when she saw who he really was? He sneered at his own thought. That was only if she chose to stay. He'd speak to Mectarn in the morning and suggest the virtues of having a capable and honorable neighbor. One who was as corporeal as the Goblins and Orcs rather than the restless spirit of a long-dead king.

That's the problem, isn't it?

Allira was corporeal, and he was nothing more than a wisp of thought and memory. A soul unmoored from a skeleton still seated upon a throne, governing nothing. With that bleak thought, he turned away from his dusty bones in the lost and forgotten throne room, refusing to look into his own empty eye sockets below the iron crown resting on his skull.

Chapter Eight

Allira sat on her normal rock waiting for the knights to arrive for their day of destruction, munching on some stew with the last of her bread. Her stores were dwindling, and she didn't have much with which to trade, so she set up snares to catch a rabbit or two for supper that night.

Despite the uncertainty about her food situation, she was relaxed. She'd slept better last night than she had since she'd arrived at the Dreadstone Tombs. No one bothered her or the horses. The wind through the trees had been peaceful, and she'd felt secure against the wall of the hills.

It was a wise choice to move closer to Josten—er, the Tombs.

She glanced around, scanning for anyone who might be able to catch the flush that heated her cheeks, but the clearing before the gate was remarkably quiet and peaceful. If she hadn't seen the people who lived within, she would've assumed the Tombs were long abandoned.

She glanced at the position of the sun. It was later than the knights usually arrived, and she wondered if they'd taken a day to nurse their wounds and strategize. Not that she wanted them to get wiser in how they'd take on the Goblins and Orcs defending their homes, but she also wouldn't mind them not coming at all.

She stretched and listened for the sounds of approaching horses, but heard nothing beyond the wind in the trees and the birds going about their chattering business.

Odd. They should be here by now.

Setting aside her bowl, she picked up the book Josten had given her and opened it. The first page was a list of the lesser-known cases and their page numbers. Allira often wondered how many of the stories were made up, fictional accounts of something mundane, but her Nanna said she'd known Torsha so Allira couldn't discount the tales entirely.

The second story was called The Case of the Candle Killer, and the title made Allira narrow her eyes. Candles weren't alive—why would killing candles make a difference? Or perhaps the killer used candles in their ritual of killing? She'd loved the stories when she was a child so she settled her mind enough to focus and read to find out which it was.

She was so invested in the story, she didn't realize it was nearly midday when Josten appeared in the clearing—a clearing curiously empty of horses. The knights had never arrived, there were no horses to watch, and she was hungry.

"Good story?" Josten smirked as he leaned against a tree in the shade.

Allira blinked a few times and scrubbed her face with her hands. "I wasn't convinced I'd like the story, but then I started reading and I totally got sucked in." She glanced around the clearing. "Have you seen the knights today? I didn't realize how late it was. They should've been here by now."

"Perhaps yesterday was too much for them."

She grimaced. "I can only hope."

"Well, since you don't have anything else to do, would you be interested in building a little?"

"Building? What kind of building?" She rose and stretched before tucking the book under her arm.

"I thought you'd like a more permanent structure for your accumulated horses."

She frowned. "But I haven't asked the Goblins and Orcs if they're okay with me being their neighbor. There's no point in putting up a fence if they don't want me around."

"I talked to the Council of Elders this morning, and they've given provisional agreement that you may stay close to the Tombs." Josten gestured for her to lead them toward her camp. "Gundri even put in a good word for you. She reminded everyone that you've never set foot inside the Tombs without invitation, and helped clear up the debris. The Council was very impressed and agreed it might be useful to have a human nearby."

"They have you."

He shrugged. "What's the phrase folks used to say? Four hands are better than two?"

She rolled her eyes. "It's okay to admit you like having the company of someone who likes to read Torsha the Bold stories so you can trade books."

He laughed. "Busted."

His grin warmed her all the way through, and she couldn't help but wonder what it would be like to spend more time with him. Sharing meals, taking care of the horses—*Those imaginary chickens I've been thinking about*—sharing a bed even, though it was way too early to be ruminating in that direction.

She cleared her throat as they entered her camp with the broken sword gate. The horses were still tied to their picket line, and she grimaced. They really needed a larger space to roam. Besides the lack of space, the horse manure was building up too close to her camp. Come high summer, the place would stink and be full of flies.

If I'm still here then. But I'd have great fertilizer for the garden.

"Yeah, it might be a good idea to build an enclosure for the horses far enough away from my sleeping space to keep the manure in check." Allira shuddered as she pointed at the piles that would need to be moved.

"Excellent. The workers should be here soon to help."

"Wait, what? What are you talking about?"

Josten pointed, and several Goblins and Orcs tramped along the wall of the Tombs toward her camp, carrying rails and a tool resembling a post-hole digger. Gundri was in the lead and she had several shovels braced across her shoulders.

"What are they doing here? Josten?"

He waved to the Orcs and Goblins. "Right, let's make a big enough enclosure for the horses to roam enough. Ulfer, make sure to clean up the manure and move it away from the stream."

The newcomers nodded and hopped to work as Allira stood there with her jaw open.

"What just happened?"

Josten shot her a grin. "I'm delegating labor to complete a task."

"But why?"

He shot her a smirk. "I just had to?"

"Keep going like that, Josten, and pretty soon folks will start looking at you like a town leader or king or something." She shook her head but didn't miss how his shoulders tightened and he swallowed visibly. "Hey, did I say something wrong? Are you okay?"

"I'm fine, just a little warm in the sun." He gave her a quick, patently fake smile as he stepped into the shade. "Why do you ask?"

"Other than the fact that you look like I accused you of stealing cookies from a cookie jar and your expression tightened with guilt, no reason." She shrugged, but still waited him out.

He laughed, but it sounded forced. "In my younger years, I did take some leadership roles, but I'm afraid I wasn't very good at them. It must be old habits coming back."

"Mmm." She nodded, but something about his explanation didn't ring true.

"Why don't you talk to Gundri about your camp? I'm sure she can suggest the best way to set it up."

She raised an eyebrow. "Are you saying you don't like the setup I have?"

"No, no, just it's not the most defensible or protected from the elements." Josten raised his hands in surrender. "One good windstorm and your tent will be visiting the horses at the end of the field."

She shot a look toward the end of the meadow where the Goblins and Orcs were already digging post holes. Biting her lip, she considered the implication of having to find her tent after gale-force winds.

"Yeah, you might be right. I really don't know how the camp would fare in rough weather."

Josten nodded sagely. "Let's talk to Gundri. She has an innate ability to set up the best and most secure camp I've ever seen."

Allira followed Josten into the clearing while the horses watched the commotion around them. She was surprised none of them spooked from the proximity to Orcs, but they seemed relaxed if watchful.

The Goblins and Orcs had secured posts halfway around the clearing and had fitted rails to the first quarter. Allira and Josten caught up with Gundri as the others started the second half, and she smiled gratefully when Josten requested her help with the camp construction.

"Anything for the Dismemberer of Dreadstone." Gundri grinned as she clapped Allira on the shoulder.

"The who?" Allira blinked.

"The Dismemberer of Dreadstone. Were you not the one who helped us peel the body parts from the armor?" Gundri nodded with satisfaction. "We all agreed that you deserved a title for the great deeds you did in the service of the Dreadstone Kingdom, and Peeler didn't sound grand enough. So, what are you looking for in a good camp?"

"Uh..." Allira followed the fierce Goblin woman, her mind a blank of astonishment. They'd given her a title. She cleared her throat to get her mind back in gear. "Stability?"

"Good." Gundri nodded as they returned to where Allira had pitched her tent. "Defensibility is another good aspect. Since we are already digging holes for posts, we can also do this for a lean-to. It will give you protection from both the wind and rain when the storms roll in. Oh." She leaned closer to Allira. "We also brought a few more things we thought you could use to decorate. I thought the broken sword made an excellent gate post."

"Really? Thank you. It just seemed like a better use of broken weapons." Allira shot a surprised look at Josten, and he just grinned. "How will you build the lean-to?"

"First, let's take your tent down and stow your things out of the way. Then we'll get the gren to cut down a few saplings for the frame. Here, I'll get this end while you take that one."

Gundri gathered up Allira's sleeping gear while Allira scrambled to pick up her personal items, and soon the tent sat empty. By the time they took the tent down, the Goblins and Orcs had almost finished the corral for the horses. Gundri called out to the bigger Orcs and directed them to find five straight saplings. Then she directed the women Goblins to gather up the best grasses for weaving ropes. Allira asked to help, and Gundri showed her how to braid the tough fibers into sturdy strands that even the Orc men couldn't break.

Josten drifted away and helped the rest of the crew work on finishing the corral and horse shelter, complete with working gate. Allira looked for him as the larger Orcs returned with five tall saplings, stripped of bark and branches, but she couldn't look long as half the corral crew left off and began working on the lean-to.

She worked with the women, whom Gundri referred to as grells, and helped them lash the sawed-off saplings into place at the corners to make a rough kiosk. Then the gren, the male Goblins and Orcs, picked up the leftover fence rails and placed them as stabilizing braces between the uprights of the kiosk using the remaining nails to hold them in place. Gundri directed the whole crew like a captain who ran the system on knowledge and experience. Even Allira fell into line when the grell told her how to weave rope or layer pine boughs for a roof over thin branches laid across the roof posts.

By the early afternoon, Allira not only had a corral with a working gate and a shelter for the horses to get out of the wind, but the manure pile had been moved downwind and her tent sat under a three-sided shelter with a fixed roof. The grells had broken off and started cooking for the whole crew on her firepit, which consequently became slightly larger and had a spit installed.

The midday meal came together faster than she expected and was surprisingly tasty. She lost track of Josten for a while as the gren and grells shared a lively discussion about who was the faster team—those on the corral or those on the shelter. There was good-natured ribbing on both sides, and Allira had an epiphany.

Humans were idiots.

The people she'd known and grown up with all thought Goblins and Orcs were nothing more than monsters, no better than beasts. The humans felt entitled to enter places 'infested' with Goblins and Orcs, robbing and killing them, disdaining them for the lack of clothing, civilization, and intelligence.

The fools couldn't be more wrong.

The gren spoke of strategy and physics when it came to construction projects. The grells were all about efficiency and innovations, making things easier to get daily tasks done. They talked about their gardens in the Tombs and how they'd gotten both the light and the water to flow where they wanted.

And yet, here they are, helping me, a human come to rob and kill them.

Her only saving grace was her choice not to enter the Tombs. But she'd held the same opinion about Orcs and Goblins before she'd seen them in action. She'd revised her thoughts over the days she'd been at the Dreadstone Caves, as the natives called them, and was determined to change the minds of all the people she knew once she returned home.

Except, Gundri and the others had done a wonderful job of making her camp semi-permanent. Would she choose to stay? Or was all this work for nothing?

Again, Allira looked around for Josten, but he'd disappeared. She frowned.

Curious.

She finished her food and set her plate on the pile meant for washing before grabbing her largest pot for washing water. She hauled it to the stream, scanning the people in the clearing for Josten's distinctive form. She found several of the gren as they carved the meat off the spit and teased each other about cooking prowess, but Josten wasn't among them.

She filled up her pot and brought it back to the fire just as Josten returned to the camp, reminding the Orcs about training maneuvers and home-building projects. The gren and grells grumbled good-naturedly and cleaned up the remains of the meal before heading back toward the Tombs. Allira set her pot on the fire to make dishwater and watched in amazement as the camp cleared out.

By the time the water started to boil, her camp was deserted, and she pulled the water off the fire to let it cool enough to be used for washing dishes. Josten remained, checking over the workgrenship of the corral and the lean-to.

She snorted. *As if the Goblins and Orcs didn't know what they were doing.*

Then she frowned. Josten would know better than her the gren and grells could do the work without supervision. What was he really doing? Was he stalling before talking to her? And if so, why?

She poured some of the hot water into the cold to make a warm bath for the dishes as she puzzled through Josten's weird behavior. Maybe he had a crush on her and didn't want to get razzed by the others.

Go on, flatter yourself, why don't you.

She grimaced as she tested the water. Maybe *she* had a crush on him and didn't want to admit it. A curious feeling of unease and excitement rattled around in her chest. A crush on Josten? That was ridiculous.

Except, he'd kept her company when there was nothing to do, helped her make a better camp somewhere away from the invaders, and brought her books to read to pass the time. What wasn't to like?

She dumped soap into the water and added the dishes so they could soak before she had to scrub them with a washcloth made from woven hard grasses. She glanced around the camp to check on Josten's progress and found him making his way back to her wash station.

"Everything look good?" She gave him a smile as she reached into her washbasin, hissing a little at the heat.

He nodded, though his expression was troubled. "Yes, the Goblins and Orcs do good work."

"I noticed. Did you see the kiosk? It's like a hotel instead of a camp."

"We wanted to be sure you're protected from the weather." He settled on a nearby rock and waved at the wash bin. "Do you want help?"

She shook her head. "Nope. I'm faster by myself. Hey, where did you go, earlier? I looked around for you, but you'd disappeared."

"Yeah, I ran back into the Caves to be sure the knights hadn't been waiting for the defenders to be elsewhere when they made today's incursion."

Allira straightened. "Were there horses in the clearing?"

"No, thank the Goddess. Apparently, the knights are taking a day off."

"I'm all for that. Hell, they could take the next year off, and just stop doing the event all together." She shook her head as she scrubbed the plates and slid them into the cool rinsing water. "I think the Goblins and Orcs should petition the local magistrate to stop the event that causes damage to their homes."

"Who would they send? The moment either of them stepped into a human village, they'd be killed for just existing." Josten scowled. "Most humans don't see them as people, only monsters."

"I've said it before—the only monsters here are the humans."

"Excluding you, of course." He smirked.

She snorted and shook her head. "Not necessarily. When I first arrived, I shared the opinions that the Goblins and Orcs were just mindless creatures. Granted, I didn't want to invade their spaces, but I didn't think them intelligent. That pretty much cements my position as a human monster."

"All evidence to the contrary. You've shown compassion and have been willing to talk to them after learning they weren't what you thought. The same can't be said for the other humans who've come to the Caves over the years." He waved to the camp and corral. "They wouldn't have done this for you if they didn't think you were worthy of it."

"Wait." She held up a soapy hand. "We both know they did this for *you*, not me. They respect *you*, and you asked them to do this, so they did."

He shrugged one shoulder. "Maybe, but they could've told me to go jump off a cliff."

She snorted again. "There's no way they'd say that to you, and you know it. But I appreciate their faith in you, and by extension, me. I really like my camp now. It's downright comfortable."

"That's true. It would be a great place to make those chocolate and fluffed sugar treats we used to make as kids."

Allira blinked. "You made s'mores when you were a kid?"

"Is that what they call them now? We always called them fluff-n-melts, and no surface remained clean after eating them." Josten grinned. "Pissed off the ones assigned cleanup duty."

Allira finished the dishes and set the rinsed plates in a pile to be dried. "Yeah, I wouldn't have been thrilled either. Speaking of which, I think one of the other knights might have the ingredients of s'mores if you want to make them."

"Oh, I can't at the moment. I need to get back to my own chores."

"Oh, okay." She tried not to let disappointment swamp her. *See, you* do *have a crush on him.* "Do you want to come by after supper tonight? I could make them then."

"I'm sorry, I can't tonight. I have other plans." He looked contrite. "But I can come by early tomorrow morning before you head off to the clearing, if that's amenable."

She found her smile somewhere. "Yeah, that would be great. So, I guess I'll see you tomorrow."

He bobbed his head as he stood. "Yes, tomorrow."

Then he was gone and she dried her dishes, wondering when she'd started missing his company.

Chapter Nine

J osten tried to ignore the voice in his head reminding him that he needed to tell Allira the truth about the Dreadstone King and himself. But he didn't want to lose the connection he had with her, or her goodwill.

And that's exactly what will happen when she finds out I'm a ghost.

It was a when question, not an if question.

He was a ghost, had been for seventy-two years, and he had no future. He scowled as he materialized in the throne room of his underground palace. The huge stone chair stood on a carved dais three steps up from the cave floor. In the seat of the chair, leaning to the left with its head bowed, was his skeleton, articulated only by magic, grinning at the floor with an iron crown on its skull. There was a sword, too, hidden in the backboard of the chair, but he rarely had to use it.

The bones and the crown were all that was left of him, and he rarely animated them unless absolutely necessary. He could, and it was frightening as hell, but he'd found less and less of a reason to make the effort over the decades. Most of the time, the Goblins and Orcs took care of the intruders, and Josten didn't have to do much.

That's all I ever seem to do—not much.

To be brutally honest, he'd been simply waiting to die for real. There was no point in staying as he was, but the magic wouldn't release him. Year after year, decade after decade, no matter the intruders and their lame-ass festival, he was stuck watching the idiots come in and disturb the residents of the caves.

They come looking for the Relic that's sitting right in front of them.

Every time the knights saw the skeleton resting on the throne, they spotted the very treasure they sought. The iron crown, plain, heavy, sharp, and rusted, with small jewels in the spikes. That was it. But so far no one thought it would be valuable enough to take, and none of the knights had tried to entertain their comrades by plucking the crown off the skeleton and setting it on their own heads.

Would that release me from this unlife?

Would the skeleton crumble into dust when the crown was lifted? Would the curse quickly transfer to the fool who took it, releasing Josten? Would the treasure-hungry fool even know he'd found the one thing they all wanted?

Josten shook his head.

"It's a wonder it's held together all these years."

He started when the mellow, soothing tones of the Goblins' holy woman disrupted his thoughts. Mectarn tilted her head just enough to glance up at him through her beaded dreads with her golden eyes.

"Did I surprise you, your Highness?"

Josten snorted. "Yes, and I'm no more a 'highness' than I am alive."

Mectarn shrugged as she settled herself on one of the collapsed columns from the throne room. "It's a habit to call you as your rank, and you're more alive now than you ever were with a physical body. I'd wager it's that knight you've met outside the caves."

He straightened. It shouldn't have surprised him that she knew about Allira, but he tried to school his expression anyway.

"She is a friend and someone who is worth talking to as the days grow long." He gave Mectarn a polite smile. "Nothing more than a companion to pass the time with."

Mectarn grunted with amusement. "Keep telling yourself that, Highness, but I've never seen you this animated or relaxed, especially with the foolhardy humans invading. There's something about this woman who has come into our domain that captures your attention. Did I hear you asked the gren and grells to help secure her horses and improve her camp?"

Josten gave a one-shouldered shrug as he turned away from the throne. "It seemed the kindest thing to do when she chose to move her camp away from the other humans. She's been collecting the horses of the dead, and couldn't keep them on a picket line. It's easiest for us to build a corral and a lean-to. I was happy to arrange it for her."

"Hmm. She must have made an impression. I understand you raided your few bookshelves to bring her one." Mectarn raised her eyebrows. "That took a fair amount of energy on your part, I'd wager, to carry a solid book all the way to her new camp, *outside* the caves. You've never made such an effort before."

"Because all the humans that ever came to Dreadstone have harmed the people here. They see them as monsters and creatures, not intelligent beings. And they kill for the promise of treasure. I need a change of view. Come with me?" Josten offered his hand to Mectarn, focusing on being solid. She took it and stood before they turned their feet toward the gardens in the caverns. "Allira never wanted to come in or harm anyone. Hell, she didn't even want to come with the others."

"A true anomaly. Why is she here, then?"

Mectarn kept pace with him, using a gnarled and polished walking stick embedded with fresh-water pearls and raw crystals found within the caverns. He suspected it was more of a wizard's staff than a walking stick, but he'd never asked about it.

"She said she was convinced to join to ensure her grandmothers' prosperity. The Town Council promised her the farm would remain in her grandmothers' possession for their lives if she joined as the thirteenth warrior of this year's farce."

"So, she's merely here to be their good luck charm, but not to wreak havoc on the people who live in the caverns? Interesting and altruistic. She's doing the bare minimum to fulfill her obligation in order to protect family." Mectarn nodded, pensive. "I can see why you're drawn to her."

Josten wanted to scoff, but many a Goblin had suffered when they didn't listen to Mectarn's wisdom, even if it wasn't what they wanted to hear. The clicking of her walking stick punctuated their progress toward the gardens as he schooled his reaction to be regretful.

He sighed. "There's no point in being drawn to her because I have no future. I'm nothing but a dusty skeleton on a stone throne with an iron crown, and a wandering ghost with the solidity of a shadow. I can't be anything more to Allira because I'm literally nothing."

Mectarn grunted again. "I think you give yourself too little credit, Highness. You just lifted me off that column." She shot him a dry look as they passed through the garden entrance. Some work had been done to repair them, but signs of damage remained. "But come, what is it you truly want now? We know what you wanted when you took the crown, but I think you have changed your mind. If you could have anything, what would it be?"

"That's a silly question."

Mectarn nodded sagely. "Yes, it is. You could use a little silly in your life. Be silly and answer the question." She bent and picked up a flower, partially wilted, from the floor of the walkway and handed it to him.

He almost allowed it to fall through his ghostly hand, but caught it almost reflexively and the delicate petals lay heavy in his palm.

Josten closed his mouth and thought carefully. Mectarn rarely asked such pointed questions. Usually, she led whoever she was talking to through a carefully laid path so they would come to the understanding they needed on their own. But this time, she didn't bother with meandering.

"I want... I want more time." He studied the flower.

She snorted. "You have all the time in the world, Highness."

"No, I want more *life* time. I want to learn how to play the harp, and tend a garden, and spend time just sitting around a fire with someone, sharing the stories of the day."

She grunted. "Can't you do that now? I mean, beyond the harp, you can learn how to tend these gardens." She gestured to the magnificent growth around them. "And you can join the gren and grells around their fires anytime you please."

"Yes, but there's no shared camaraderie. Not really. They all see me as the Dreadstone King-that-was, His Highness, not a friend or a companion." He shook his head and waved at the Goblins tending the gardens. "I'm someone to serve because they knew me from the stories as my rank."

"I think they see you as more than that, Highness." Mectarn settled herself on a mossy rock. "But that's not answering my question. What do you truly want?"

"I want a second chance." The words burst from him, unbidden, and he blinked in surprise.

She raised her eyebrows. "A second chance at what, Highness?"

"A second chance at a real life. One without constant violence to make ends meet. And one where I'm only responsible for me and my loved ones, not a whole kingdom."

"I see. Do you have a loved one in mind?"

To his surprise, his cheeks heated. She *had* led him exactly where he needed to go. He looked away and focused on the cascade of a waterfall that brought irrigation to the gardens.

"Not... entirely."

She snorted. "Be honest, Josten. There's no use lying to yourself."

He tightened his hands into fists. "I don't know her well enough to say for sure. And as I am, there's no hope of it. But if I had more time, I would spend it with Allira, to see if there's a real friendship."

"Still hedging your bets, I see." Mectarn shook her head, her dreads clacking. "You have all the time in the world, Josten. You're a ghost, so use that time to build something important."

"What's the point? I'm dead. I can't give her what she wants."

"Do you *know* that for sure? Do you even know what she wants for her future?"

He opened his mouth to answer, but closed it with a grimace. "No."

"Hmm, perhaps you might find that out before you make rash decisions about anyone's future." Mectarn smiled. "There's an old Orckian saying that goes, 'The more you know, the wiser you become.' I think it's time for you to increase your wisdom, Highness."

She nodded to him and rose, taking measured steps toward her own dwelling, leaving him to his thoughts. Josten wanted to believe all it would take was asking a few questions and the path to any future would be laid before him. But experience had taught him that humans didn't take kindly to either of his forms—ghostly or skeletal—and he didn't want Allira to panic when she recognized either.

True to his word, Josten was in Allira's camp early the next morning. He'd wanted to share the s'mores with her more than anything, but he wasn't ready to reveal his ghostly status yet. But he could build something important, as Mectarn had said. Maybe in his time with Allira he could figure out a way to tell her he wasn't just an old knight who lived near the Tombs. Soon, all the other knights would either leave on their own or die within the Tombs, and Allira would head back to her grandmothers' farm. He knew the end was coming and he'd be out of time to strengthen the tenuous friendship they had.

Allira emerged from her tent, scrubbing her face with her hands, and he was struck by how beautiful she was in the dawn light. She stretched and her shirt tightened against her breasts, reminding Josten that he might be dead, but he wasn't *dead* dead.

"Oh, glory, I didn't see you there, Josten!" Allira gasped and pressed a hand to her chest. "How long have you been here?"

"Not long. I just arrived a bit ago." He gave her an easy shrug. "Did you sleep well?"

She nodded as her jaw cracked with a yawn. "Yeah. Best sleep I've had in a while, actually. Had a crazy dream where I met the Dreadstone King, and he warned me to be kind to the Orcs and Goblins with whom I shared the Tombs."

His gut sank. "Really? That sounds scary."

She shrugged. "It was a little, I guess, but since I like the grells and gren I've met, I wasn't too worried."

"What...what did the king look like?" Why the hell was he asking that?

She frowned a little as she started her fire and filled a pot with water. "Imposing. I couldn't see his face, but he wore a great iron crown on his head and his voice thundered in the caverns. And he had a huge sword strapped to his back." She shivered theatrically. "I bet he was terrifying while alive."

Josten nodded and grunted a response, but he couldn't find anything coherent to say. She'd described him to a T, and he definitely couldn't tell her she'd seen his guardian aspect, minus the skeletal remains with the green flames flickering from his eye sockets.

Yeah, I should totally show her that for our first real date.

"I saw a painting of him once." She glanced up at Josten with a rueful smile.

"Oh yes? What did he look like?"

Allira checked the water in the pot. "A little like you, actually, but taller, and without the silver in his hair. Plus he wasn't smiling. He looked hard and ruthless."

Josten wanted to tell her he'd grown as a man and a king, ironically after dying. But the words stuck in his throat and he couldn't spit them out. Instead, he turned his attention to the book he'd brought for her.

"Are you enjoying the book?"

She shot him a confused look, but the water boiled and she turned to attend it.

"Oh. Yeah, it's been pretty good. Let me just get my tea together and we can go check if the knights have returned."

The last thing he wanted to do was watch other people's horses while they raided the homes of his people, but she'd agreed to it and her honor required her to keep her word. He stood back as she prepared her tea and banked the fire. She checked on the horses in the corral, particularly her charcoal gray named Javalina, before she picked up her tea mug and nodded to him.

They set off toward the clearing without a word, but Josten kept thinking about her honor and what they were preparing to do. Fortunately, the knights hadn't arrived by the time they stepped into the clearing before the gate. The area was clear and quiet, the wind rustling the trees and shrubs.

"Huh." Allira glanced up at the sun. "A bit late. Shouldn't they be here by now?" She swept the clearing with her gaze. "I mean, don't they want all the daylight for their campaign?"

"I don't know." He frowned as he scanned the clearing. "I have no interest in encouraging them. Speaking of which, why do you come here to watch their horses?"

She grimaced. "I promised."

"Even if it enables them to rain hell on the people who live here?"

She opened her mouth, but paused. "You make a good point. I guess I could come back in the afternoon and see which horses are left." She rubbed the back of her neck. "I didn't think about helping them. I just wanted something to do instead of going into the Tombs."

"If it's something to do you want, I can help you spar, or we could gather tubers and herbs for tonight's supper." Josten tipped his head with a smirk. "You know, if you're bored or something."

Allira laughed. "Yeah, okay, sparring sounds good. I've been feeling lazy these days." She sipped her tea and stared meditatively at the gate. "But I'd like to finish my tea first. And eat."

"Anything else?" he asked dryly.

"Well as long as we're wishing, I'd like a stove to cook on and a pantry full of food."

He snorted. "I don't think I have a stove on hand, but we might be able to convince the gren and grells to provide a pantry of sorts."

"Are you sure they want to help the Dismemberer of Dreadstone?" Allira turned back toward her camp. "Let's at least go back to camp to get my sword, that way we're prepared."

"Oh ye of little ingenuity. Surely we can find weapons at hand. Show me what you've got."

She rolled her eyes. "Tea and breakfast first. One doesn't do well at war on an empty stomach, which I *know* the Wraiths taught you. My Mima said that all the time."

Josten narrowed his eyes. "Very well, Dismemberer. But don't take too long. You said you were feeling lazy and we can't have that."

"Just be glad I'm not hangry. Then we'd really have a problem." She shot him a smirk. "But come on. I'll even share my hot oatcakes with you."

"Oooh, with honey and cinnamon? They were my favorites."

She shot him a bemused look but nodded. "How else are you supposed to eat them?"

He laughed to cover up his slip. Hopefully, she hadn't caught how the oatcakes used to be something he loved...when he was alive. He followed her into her camp and settled on one of the stumps while she puttered around the spit, making her pan-fried oatcakes.

He couldn't smell them, but his mind filled in the blanks as she dropped the batter into the pan and flipped the cakes. Oh, how he wished he could share in them with her, but he'd have to be content with her own enjoyment of them.

When she slid them onto a board for eating, she offered it to him. "Would you like some? You came here awfully early."

"Thank you, but no. I'm just waiting on you to get your breakfast before we start to spar."

"Yeah, yeah, I'm working on it." She rolled her eyes but tucked into her breakfast and he tried not to be jealous.

He tried to think of something to talk about to take his mind off the food he couldn't taste, but Allira beat him to it.

"I can't believe I didn't think about what I was doing." When he raised his eyebrows, she grimaced. "Enabling the monsters hurting the people. For the first few days, fine. I didn't understand what I was doing. But now? Let their flipping horses get eaten by predators. Serves them right for invading someone's home."

"You could think of it as protecting your investment. After all, the horses left by the dead men become yours."

She laughed as she finished her meal. "That's a morbid way of looking at it, but you're not wrong. I might just keep checking on them to make sure they're healthy. The horses, not the men." She brushed off her hands and picked up her plate. "Okay, I'm ready. I'll let the pan cool before we clean it. Where would you like to spar? And with what?"

"You can't spar with wooden staffs or spears?" He rose and moved toward the remaining supplies left over from building her camp. "Have you forgotten how to use what's at hand?"

He bent down and retrieved two long poles left by the gren when they constructed the corral. It took all of his concentration to solidify his hands enough to grasp them, but he managed it, and tossed one to Allira. She caught it and held it up with raised eyebrows.

"You weren't kidding. Aren't these a little long for staff fighting?" She hefted the pole, and it moved awkwardly in her grip.

He raised an eyebrow. "Do you have more suitable weapons?"

She smirked and tossed the pole back onto the ground. "Of course, I do. Come on. The knights left all their extras when they died."

He dropped the rail and followed her to where she'd stashed the other knights' usable weapons. Sure enough, there were two staffs, carved with ornate designs and tipped with steel caps.

"Ahh, now those are the perfect weapons." He grinned as she tossed one of the staffs at him. Again, he had to concentrate to make sure it didn't fall through him, and he twirled it like he used to do when he was young and cocky.

Who am I kidding? I'm still cocky.

"Oooh, nice moves there, Joss." The nickname sounded natural and well-worn, and a thrill ran up Josten's back. "Gonna use it when we come to blows?"

"You'll just have to see." He grinned as he moved into the open space beside the camp. "Ready?"

"Bring it."

Before he could get into a guard position, Allira was moving. Her staff flashed out toward his head, and he dodged, glad he wasn't completely solid because she would've clocked him, hard. He lost his grin and focused on her moves, letting the rhythms of her staff work remind him of his own training.

They moved around the open space in front of her camp, trading blows and dodging strikes. He fell into the old habits he'd developed as a young mercenary, training for war. Allira didn't have some of the tricks, but she adapted on the fly, and he was very impressed with her skills.

He knocked her down, finally, and she grunted as she hit the dirt but rolled to her feet.

"Nice. Let's take a break. You got some skills, woman." He bent over and feigned being out of breath.

"You, too. I can see why they used you in the Wraiths. I learned a couple things today."

"Wait 'til you've seen my sword work. I was better at that than at staffs."

She raised an eyebrow as she grabbed her canteen. "Boasting, now?"

"It's not boasting if I can back it up." He gave her a tired smile. "Give me a few moments and you can test the theory."

She laughed, wiping her mouth. "I'll hold you to that." She straightened and set her staff aside. "Some of these are well-made. If I don't have my sword, they'll come in very handy."

He dropped the second staff next to hers. "They're good for keeping enemies at bay, true, but you have to have them nearby to ward off the worst."

She nodded slowly as she retrieved her sword. "Sounds like you're speaking from experience."

He grimaced. "I am. We were on a campaign to protect some landowner's estate and the surrounding villages, and I'd just come off the first watch of sentry duty. I was beat and dead on my feet, so I left the staff with the next sentry and hit the sack. The raiders we'd been contracted to take down decided that night was the one to overwhelm our defenses because..." He spread his hands. "They got a wild hair up their butts? No clue, but those of us asleep woke to find assholes coming through our camp, intent on killing us. The staffs were too far away, but I kept my daggers and sword with me. I was a little slow and got some slashes to my arms for my troubles, but I ended up killing my attackers with my dagger and bare hands."

He didn't like remembering those events, but they had taught him to be vigilant, and prepared.

"Damn. Talk about a lesson hard-earned." Allira shook her head and stretched her arms behind her, pushing out her chest.

Josten enjoyed her taut shirt against her breasts and had to look away before his body betrayed his admiration. He cleared his throat.

"So, yeah, I prefer using my sword." *In more ways than in battle.* "You ready to spar with blades?" He bent over and reached behind the rails, summoning his blade. When he rose, he held a two-handed broad sword with a fuller down the long blade and a double horse heads with emerald eyes as the pommel.

"Where did that come from? I didn't see it on you earlier." She raised her eyebrows.

"Oh, uh..." He thought fast. "I deposited it here just in case we wanted to work on your moves since you'd mentioned being bored." She had, hadn't she, prior to this morning? He hoped his explanation sounded plausible.

"Huh. It's pretty, I'll give you that. Did you fight with it back in the day?"

He tilted the blade, glancing at it. "Yup. This has saved my ass more times than I can remember."

"Heh. Nice green-eyed horses. They got names?" She held up her own sword, a slimmer blade with a leather-wrapped hilt and a simple brass disk pommel. Except, when she turned the blade, the disk held markings he couldn't quite interpret.

"Not that they've told me, although one belongs to the Horseman War and the other, to Death."

"That tracks. Both are useful for your line of work." She raised her blade. "Ready?"

"Always."

She didn't let the word finish before she was moving, and he had to admit, she was fast, even after their earlier sparring match. She didn't use large sweeping moves, but short, efficient strokes and jabs that made him reevaluate his own fighting style. Her blade was shorter and lighter, which made it fast, but he had a longer reach, both with his height and the broadsword's length.

He let her drive him around the clearing to get a sense of her fighting style, watching how she moved and what tells she might have. She didn't have many, though, and he found himself having to defend against her flurry of blows more than he expected.

They were so evenly matched, their bout didn't end until he lost his balance when he stepped on a rock, and with it, his concentration. Her sword sailed through his as if he wasn't there, and he came down hard on his side. It seemed strange he could feel the impact with the ground as a ghost, but he landed with a grunt and Allira stood over him with her blade at his throat.

"Yield?" She panted, but the sword didn't waver.

"I yield." He nodded and dropped his own blade on the ground. "I must say I'm grateful you chose not to come into the Tombs with the other humans. The gren and grells would've been hard-pressed to deal with you."

She nodded, her expression solemn. "I never said I was incapable. I just had no need of the 'glory' I would supposedly gain from this backwards endeavor." She held out her hand to help him up.

Josten forced himself to concentrate on grasping her hand and she hauled him to his feet. She gave him a nod and headed into her camp to clean and stow her blade. He took her distraction to send his sword back to the scabbard in which it had hung since he'd 'died.'

And that was all it took to remind him of Mectarn's suggestion and the problem of his future.

What future?

But Mectarn had pointed out he'd get nothing if he didn't ask for more information, so he ignored his impulse to fade back into his twilight existence, and went to see what all Allira needed to do around camp.

Chapter Ten

Something had changed. Allira could feel it in the way Josten interacted with her after their sparring bouts. He was more attentive and willing to listen to her.

So, all it took was me beating on him with a weapon to get through to him? Great.

But he helped her clean up the weapons left from the knights, feed the horses, and make a midday meal. He was surprised by her knowledge of plant lore and asked if she'd taken herblore or medicine training.

She shrugged as she put tubers in one of the cast iron pots with oil and herbs to roast in the coals of the fire. "A little. Most of the herblore I learned was from the camp cooks because my Nanna told me I could always make something tasteless taste good with the right herbs. Plus, it paid to help the cooks because they always gave me extras." She grinned as Josten laughed.

"But I only learned the basics of medicinal herbs. Clotwort for slowing bleeding; lavender for burns and scratches; bitterpods to kill infection, stuff like that."

Josten nodded at the tubers. "How long will those take to cook?"

She narrowed her eyes. "Uhm, almost an hour. Why?"

"Grab a basket. Let me show you some of the herbs that grow around the Tombs that the Goblins have seeded for use."

"Ugh, really?" She gave him a pouty look. "I hated gathering herbs for the camp. They always made my hands smell, particularly the bitterpods, and I couldn't wash it off for days."

"Come on." He gave her an indulgent smile. "I'll help you find more of your cooking herbs so you can make a gourmet meal out of dried meat and flatbread."

She followed him, grumbling, but she couldn't tell him no. He looked too happy to show her the treasures around his home. She'd given up wondering where he lived, but she had no doubt it was near enough to the Tombs for the denizens to know him well, and respect his company. And she liked to be included in the respect the Orcs and Goblins offered Josten. She finally felt included, accepted despite how she'd come to stay there.

They gathered cooking herbs, and he taught her how to dry them to keep their potency longer than just a few days. His suggestions reminded her of how her grandmothers did things, and she wondered if he'd had the same teacher. But he'd moved on to the next herb before she could ask.

Despite going through the forest to conduct her least-favorite chore, she loved spending time with Josten, trading fighting campaign and cooking stories. She found him to be a lover of the oatcakes she'd made that morning, as well as ginger cakes with candied bits of the bitter root to chew on. He told her a funny story of trading the rescue of exotic goods from raccoons for two barrels of the sweet treats. Josten had her holding her sides from laughing so hard.

Back at camp, he helped her put together the best spiced rice and flatbread meal she'd ever eaten. After they shared the meal, he read some of her book to her while she did the dishes and stored the leftover food for supper that night. His melodic voice settled into her mind and heart, warming them both in ways she'd never thought could happen. She could listen to him recite the Seven Steps of Becoming a Knight and she'd be happy for days.

When the westering sun sank behind the Tombs, Josten took her to a new portion of the forest to show her the night-blooming flowers and the exotic critters that fed on them. Dartflies with electric blue wings that left light blurs against the black; tiny dragons with long tails that glowed with neon yellow and orange scales in alternating patterns; small skittering scampers with their banner tails that one only saw darting down a hole or under a bush.

The whole forest lit up in the reflected light of the stars and moon, hiding both predator and prey.

"This is amazing." Allira spun slowly in a circle. "How have I never seen this before?"

"These plants only grow in pockets near Orc settlements."
Josten waved at the surrounding beauty. "There's something
about their excrement that fertilizes them and keeps them blooming."

Allira wrinkled her nose. "Are you saying these plants only grow
in Orc shit?"

He nodded. "Yes, but only once it's been watered down and
filtered through the porous rocks of the Tombs. The elders of the
Matriarchy figured out they could cultivate these secret pockets
of night-blooming plants away from human villages to bring the
magical creatures back to their enclaves. Those magical creatures
in turn provide not only an increase in the energy the medicine
women use to heal and protect their people, but also a reduction
in the amount of excrement produced by an enclave."

"Wait, wait. The plants grow in shit and attract the critters that
eat the shit, too? Ew."

"It's disgusting to think about, but everything is used and recy-
cled so nothing is wasted, even the waste." Josten raised an eyebrow. "How have humans dealt with human excrement in their
villages and settlements?"

"Uh, well, I never really thought about it. Burn it, I guess?"

He nodded. "Right. It can't be reused. It's not possible because
it doesn't sustain anything else. But the Orcs have a life-partnership
with other species. If Orcs die out, so, too, do these other species.
From waste comes beauty and life."

They sat in silence for a while after that, sharing the space and
the beauty of the bioluminescent life around them. Allira had a

new appreciation for the Orcs and the species they supported. She couldn't believe the diversity and color long after the sun had gone down, and she wanted to keep such pockets of magic alive. There had to be a way to stop the humans from hunting Orcs and Goblins, and to live in relative peace.

She turned to Josten to ask if he had any ideas and found him bathed in the light from the dartflies. He appeared almost translucent, as if she turned her head just right, she might actually see through him. She frowned and focused on him, trying to tell if she could see the dartfly streaks through him or if was just a trick of the little insects' speed.

She suddenly yawned and looked again, but the translucency had faded and he appeared as solid as the stones of the Tombs behind them.

"You're tired. We should get you to bed." Josten moved closer to her and touched her elbow.

See, he's solid. I was just imagining the translucency.

"Yeah, that's probably a good idea."

Too bad he's not coming to bed with me.

She stumbled at the idea of having Josten beside her, his hard body touching hers.

"Are you all right?" His hand was back on her elbow.

"Yeah, yeah. I'm good. Must've found a root or something." She flashed a smile, though it felt more like a quick baring of teeth as she tried to get her wayward libido reined in.

Where the hell was the sentiment coming from? She'd never felt this kind of connection with any of the men she'd worked with for her whole life. No one sparked her fancy, and she'd started to wonder if perhaps she was either interested in women or no one at all. She could admit Josten was attractive in a physical way, but that had never appealed to her before.

She still wrestled with the new direction of her thoughts as they came within sight of her camp. Someone had thoughtfully lit two lanterns with frosted glass panels to keep the light soft.

"Wow, where did the lanterns come from?"

"I asked the grells who fed the horses tonight to light them so we could see the night blooming plants." Josten gave her a warm smile.

Heat curled through her and up her cheeks, and she hoped he couldn't see it in the soft light. "So, you planned this, then?"

"Spending the evening with you? Yes, I daresay I did." He nodded and took her hand, weaving his fingers with hers. "I truly like being with you, Allira. You're the most engaging person I've been with in a long time. Ever, really. I wanted—still want—more time with you."

Allira opened her mouth to be flippant, but the look on his face suggested he meant every word. "I've enjoyed the time we've spent together a lot, too, Joss."

"Not interested in more?" His smile dipped.

"No, no, I'm *very* interested in more, I just wanted you to know I appreciated the time you've spent." She squeezed his fingers. "It's pretty late. Do you want some...tea while we read more of the book you brought me?"

"Tea sounds great." He smiled as she released him and stepped through the gate into the camp.

She filled her kettle with water from the stream and built up the fire enough to let the kettle boil, trying to ignore the excited flutter in her chest for the sweetness developing between them. Perhaps she would have the courage to ask him what he would do after the remaining knights had either died off or gone home.

"Speaking of spending more time, what are your plans for after the event is over?" She grabbed the book and settled on one of the stumps hear the fire pit.

"I was going to ask you the same thing." Josten sat on another stump. "What are *your* plans?"

She shrugged and ignored the little flutter of unease. "I don't honestly know. I have three things pulling at me that need decisions."

He grunted in encouragement to continue.

She sighed. "There are things I *need* to do, things I *should* do, and things I *want* to do."

"Hm, I've been in that sort of situation. Tell me the things you need to do first."

She set the book aside and poked at the fire with a stick. "I need to return to my grandmothers' farm to let them know I've survived and make sure the deal I made with the Capstone Creek Town Council for being their thirteenth warrior is upheld. But I don't want to get stuck there. That said, I don't really want to be a mercenary anymore, traveling from place to place, fighting someone else's battles for coin. I'm too old for that shit."

Josten laughed. "I hear you there. So, what are the things you *should* do?"

She wished the kettle would boil as she scrubbed her knees with her hands. "I *should* go home to my grandmothers' place and work with them on the farm. I can do it, I have the skills and knowledge to help out, and they aren't getting any younger."

He nodded. "Valid reasons, for sure. All that considered, what do you *want* to do?"

Allira took her time answering, thinking of all the pros and cons on making a new life for herself before she met his gaze across the fire.

"I *want* to let my grandmothers know I'm all right and healthy before I return here to run my little garden and keep the horses. I'd even consider those kid birthday parties, and war horsey rides." She licked her lips nervously. "Do you think that's even a possibility?"

"You want to come back to the Tombs?" Josten's eyebrows went up. "Why?"

She shrugged one shoulder as she let her gaze slide out to where the lanterns glowed in the darkness. "I like it here. It's peaceful and quiet. The only one I'm beholden to is myself and the critters I care for." She let her gaze return to his face. "And you're here."

"You shouldn't base your decision on me."

"I'm not." Allira shook her head, her unease sparking again. Didn't he like her? She thought they were developing something special. "You're just one more reason to keep me here. As I said, I like it here, and I like the Goblins and Orcs I've met. They make great neighbors. Hell, maybe I could do something like teach other humans not to hate people based on old fears and appearance. Not that I want more human neighbors anywhere close."

He laughed, but it sounded forced. "Are you sure you'd like me around?"

She threw out her hands. "Didn't you *just* tell me you wanted more time with me?"

"Yes, yes, I did, and I *do*. I just have some odd quirks that might change your mind about me."

She took a deep breath to keep from overreacting in the wrong direction. *Remember to find patience, minhra. Jumping before you know everything you need guarantees you'll land wrong.*

"I know we haven't known each other that long, but I've enjoyed the time we've had together and I'm interested in seeing where this goes. Would you be interested in that?" She met his gaze across the flames, and waited, her unease ramping up.

To her surprise, she swore he blushed, though the flickering of the flames made it difficult to tell. He rubbed his hands together in a nervous gesture and glanced down before he straightened his shoulders with a deep breath.

"I'm...very interested in that. I'm just not very good at personal relationships of any kind." He rubbed the back of his neck. "I'm way out of practice."

"Practice is the keyword here. Anyone can practice. I'm not asking for a marriage proposal, Josten. I just thought we had a nice friendship-plus thing going on, and I wanted it to continue." It was her turn to rub the back of her neck. "But I get it. We're relative strangers, and I came here with a band of blood-thirsty savages bent on causing harm. I wouldn't want to get to know me better, either."

He kept rubbing his hands together. "We both know you're not like the men who come to cause damage. But there are things...about me that make relationships difficult."

She dropped her chin. "What have we been doing this past sennight?"

"Getting to know each other?"

"Right. How is that not a relationship, at least in the making?" She set her chin on her woven hands and raised her eyebrows.

"I..." He heaved a deep breath. "I'm really out of my depth here."

"Okay, I'll make this simple for you. Do you want to continue what we have here, friendship-plus?" She didn't bother to give him an or-option.

He nodded. "Yes, very much."

"Okay, then." She took the kettle off the fire and added the tea to let it steep. "Don't worry so much about how this *should* go, and just focus on how you *want* it to go. I mean, we were just talking about shoulds and wants a bit ago, right?"

He snorted. "Yes, we were. And you said you wanted to stay here."

"I do. I'm done being a mercenary, but I don't want to be a farmer except for my own garden." She poured tea into a mug and held it up with her raised eyebrows. He nodded his head so she poured another cup and set the kettle aside. He took the mug when she handed it to him. "I'm ready for something different."

"This would definitely be that."

"What?"

Josten schooled his expression into polite interest. "Hmm?"

"What did you say?" Allira narrowed her eyes.

"Oh, nothing." He cradled the mug in his hands as if it didn't burn. "If you want to stay, I can always ask Mectarn, the shaman of the Goblins to see if she's agreeable. There haven't been any human settlements within 300 leagues for decades."

"Except for you." She sipped her tea.

"Yeah, but I don't count." He waved her statement away. "I've been here longer than them. But that just means my opinion carries some weight if I say I'm okay with you staying."

She set her mug aside and moved to a closer stump. "And *are* you okay with me staying?"

He focused his pale green gaze on her and smiled. "I'm very okay with you staying here."

She fell into his gaze and wondered what it would be like to kiss him. She even leaned forward in hopes he'd meet her halfway, but he blinked and sat back just enough to make her realize he'd essentially said no. Heat burned in her cheeks, and she cleared her throat as she straightened.

"Uh, so yeah, that's good." She picked up her mug of tea to have something to do.

"I'm sorry, Allira. I'm not very good at this." Contrition looked good on him, but it still pissed her off.

She gave herself a few moments to gather her thoughts. "Listen, Joss. You're sending me seriously mixed messages here, and I'm starting to think you just like toying with people. And I'm really not into that. So just give it to me straight. Do you want to work on this relationship?"

He nodded sharply. "I do."

"And you want me to stay around the Tombs once the festival is over for the year?"

"Yes, very much."

"And do you want to kiss me right now?"

Pain filtered through his expression. "I...do."

"But?" She raised her eyebrows and hoped he wouldn't notice how white her knuckles were around her mug.

"But there are things you still need to know about me, and... I'm not quite ready to talk about them." The contrition sharpened, but under it she could read his refusal to reveal whatever secret he was withholding.

She let out her breath in a long sigh. "Okay. Does it have anything to do with me being human?"

"No, not at all." He shook his head. "For once this is me, me, all about me."

Allira barked a surprised laugh. "Well, since it's all about you, how 'bout you read to *me* tonight, so I can bask in the greatness of your voice?"

He grinned and held his hand out for the book. "Done. I shall lull you into a stupor with my reading ability."

She handed him the book, and he scooted closer to the fire to get better light. Then he cracked it open and began to read.

"The Curse of the Rusty Crown." Josten choked and started to cough.

"Are you all right? Here, let me get you some water." Allira rose and grabbed her water skin, but he waved her off.

"No, no, I'm okay. Just breathed in a little spittle. I'm fine." He thumped his chest with his fist and gave her a wan smile. "It's all good."

She shot him a worried look, but he opened the book again and continued reading, only clearing his throat every now and again. As the story unfolded, she let herself relax into his deep, mellow voice, and he hadn't been wrong about lulling her into a state of relaxation. Okay, he'd said 'stupor,' but it was similar. And wonderful. Hell, she could have listened to him read the birth and death registries of Capstone Creek and been entertained.

When she started to nod with sleep, Josten broke off reading with a laugh. "I think I'm putting you to sleep. Is the story that boring?"

"No, no, I'm..." She yawned wide enough to crack her jaw. "I'm enjoying it."

"Uh-huh. Come on, sleepy head. Let's get you to bed. We can read more tomorrow." He rose with the book under his arm and held out his hand to help her up.

She took his hand and tried not to notice how strong, yet gentle it was.

Imagine how that strength would feel on my body.

She smiled as she stumbled to her bedroll and practically fell into it. "I'm so tired."

"I know, Allira. You should get some rest." Josten crouched beside her tent and pulled off her boots.

"You're not going to stay and read to me some more?" She pouted, but she really wanted him to stay longer.

"I can't tonight, but I'll be back tomorrow." He tucked her into her blankets and slid her sword closer to her bed. "Remember to keep this nearby."

"If you were here with me, I wouldn't need it." She yawned again and settled her face against the pillow.

He laughed, but she could've sworn it was forced. "Oh, so I'm just your walking, talking blade, am I?"

"Yeah, I'm good with that." Sleep sucked her down and she let herself fade.

Chapter Eleven

Josten stood for a few minutes outside Allira's tent, arguing with himself. On the one hand, she'd asked him to stay, and he really *wanted* to stay with her. On the other, he still hadn't told her who or what he was.

She wants me to stay!

I can't stay, because I'm just a ghost.

Yeah, a ghost who doesn't need sleep, so what's the harm?

The harm is she doesn't know who I am.

It always came back to that one little detail. He'd meant to tell her when she'd cornered him about their relationship, but he hadn't been ready to rock their fragile foundation. She'd given hints that she wanted to be intimate, and glory knew, he wanted that more than he'd wanted anything in a long time. But fear held him back.

And the fact that I'm not really corporeal.

Which he hadn't told her about, either.

He scowled and checked the camp to make sure everything was secure before leaving the book just outside her tent. Then he headed back to the Tombs. He nodded to the few Orc sentries he passed, making a note to ask them if they'd seen the human invaders in the last couple of days, but he was in no mood to be sociable. Between Allira's advances and his own cowardice, he needed some time to get his dreck together.

He retreated to the waterfall in the back of the Tombs where the Origin River poured from the Dreadstone Hills and carved out the caves that had become the Caverns. He'd discovered it several years after he'd taken the throne, donning the cursed iron crown, and sealing his fate to be undead.

But the story of The Curse of the Rusty Crown had revealed a secret he hadn't known. Apparently, Torsha the Bold had come across the iron crown, long before he had, and discovered that the wearer only had to atone for the wrongs committed in life to be freed from the curse. At least, that was how it worked in her story.

"For those who don the Rusty Crown
It grants the heart's desire
It offers power, wealth, and land
It gives the soul eternal fire.
The Crown picks only those in need,
Who carry the perception of lack,
It offers the wearer the gift of time
To find wealth of heart to give back.
But if the lessons are not quickly learned
And the wearer makes no change,

Then time means nothing, life goes on
And the wearer forever remains.
The Crown's gifts are dearly bought,
It requires atonement in trade,
For all the actions the wearer has wrought
Only in kindness are the debts repaid."

He gazed at the waterfall, ceaselessly pouring into the pool at its base.

I have too many things to atone for.

Sighing, Josten settled in his favorite spot where he could see both the waterfall and the entrance to the Origin Cave, and tried to relax. While he rarely needed sleep, when he sat near the waterfall, the constant sound let his mind settle, and answers came to him with more clarity.

And the Mother knows I need more clarity right now.

But instead of answers to his predicament, the vision that coalesced in his mind was of Allira's camp, glowing gently in the light of her lanterns. Instead of her tent under the lean-to, the whole structure had been expanded upon to create an open-concept home, including a deck with cushions and blankets, and tall potted plants like he'd seen in Mectarn's cavern.

"Josten? Is everything okay?" Allira appeared, dressed in a white nightshift that came only to her knees and hugged her full breasts in lace.

"Yes, I just wanted to..." He trailed off, not sure why he'd come back to her camp, which didn't look like her camp at all. "Get laid?"

Allira laughed. "Is that a question?"

"Uh, yes? No? I don't know." Great, now he sounded like a babbling moron.

She stepped closer and looked him up and down. "Well, you're certainly dressed for something. I love the outfit." She waved at him, and he glanced down.

He wore one of his old night tunics, deep red with gold embroidery at collar, cuffs, and hems. On his feet were a pair of leather sandals he used for wondering around the palace. They were old, scuffed, and tattered, but they were comfortable and quiet so he wouldn't wake the servants when he couldn't sleep.

"What brings you back out here? Would you like some tea?" She held up her kettle.

"No, thank you." He cleared his throat and took a deep breath. "I came to work on our relationship a little more. I, uh, wanted to... take you up on your earlier offer."

She closed the distance between them and placed her hand on his chest. It burned straight through his clothes and sent all the blood to his cock in visceral awareness.

"Which offer was that?"

"The one to kiss you." He swallowed hard. "That's what I saw in your expression before I read aloud to you, right?"

She tilted her head with a smile. "Yes, that's true. Are you gonna do more than just kiss me?"

"Uh..." His mind blanked as all the blood made his cock swell to rigidity.

Allira grinned. "Are you always this hesitant?"

"No, dammit, I just don't want to screw this up. It's too important to me." He reached up and ran his hand through her hair. "*You're* too important to me, Allira."

"You won't screw this up if you kiss me, Joss." She patted his chest with a challenge in her eyes.

He raised his other hand to cup her cheek as he tilted his head and brushed his lips across hers. Electric pleasure surged through their connection and zipped down his back, making his nipples stand on end. He moaned and slid his tongue along the seam of her lips, begging for entrance. When she opened her mouth and tangled her tongue with his, his mind blanked white with pleasure.

She pressed her breasts against his chest and wrapped one arm around him, pulling him closer. The other hand reached down to grasp his ass to bring his aching cock against the source of her sweet heat. He damn near lost his mind when she rubbed her core against his stiff shaft.

"Oh, sweet glory, Allira. You're making it difficult to be a gentleman." He rested his head against hers as he tried to catch his breath.

"I don't want the gentleman tonight, Joss. I want the lover who will satisfy me."

She gave him a challenging grin as she stepped back. He immediately missed the searing heat of her core against his cock as she took one of his hands.

"Come to bed with me."

He shivered with anticipation, but he had to be sure. "Are you sure? You don't know everything yet."

She dragged him to her bedroom lit up with lanterns, and ran her hand over his aching shaft through his night tunic. "This right here is all I need to know about you. Well, that and if you know how to use your tongue for more than talking."

He growled as arousal shot through him with her challenge. "Be careful what you wish for, Allira. I was known in my time as one of the greatest lovers of the land."

While that had been true, he'd wondered if it was the ladies' way of placating a king's ego rather than truth. But Allira grinned and sat on the bed with her legs spread.

"Hmm, I'm willing to chance it." She pulled her night-ie—knightie?—over her head and dropped it on the floor before bracing herself on her hands. "Like what you see, Josten?"

Sweet Mother goddess of the realm.

The freckles on her face weren't the only ones. They cascaded down either side of her neck in a golden-brown flood and outlined each full breast. Her areolas matched their color. More freckles ran from below her breasts in a thick mass down her ribs to merge above her mound and the dark nest of curls there. The hair glinted in the light and his cock flexed as he realized just how wet she was. A hint of rosy pink showed through her curls as her clit peeked beyond her labia.

"Josten?"

He blinked. "Yes, yes, I very much like what I see. But I need to taste your luscious pussy before I make my final determination."

She ran a hand down her body until she slid her fingers into her wet curls. "Oh yes, I'd like that. But first, I need to see you completely. Show me your body, and I'll give you my pussy."

Josten couldn't divest himself of his clothes fast enough. He threw them on the floor beside the bed and spread his arms as he met her hot gaze. Then he turned in a circle, allowing her to take in not only his rampant cock, but his tight ass and muscled shoulders.

"Does this meet with your approval, my lady?" He turned around and damn near swallowed his tongue as she stroked herself with her fingers.

"Oh glory, yes. You're more than I'd hoped for." She sat up and reached for him. "Bring me that cock so I can suck on it like the treat it is."

He laughed as he came closer. "I'll give you my cock, but not yet. Right now, I want to taste your pussy on my tongue."

She whimpered and licked her lips as he gently pushed her flat on the bed.

"Keep your legs spread for me, Allira." He knelt between her taut thighs, marked with a few scars from the years she'd been a warrior, and ran his fingers over them. "You're so beautiful. Each mark shows your strength and ability."

She snorted and looked down her body at him. "I'd think those scars show how many times I didn't get out of the way fast enough."

"Oh no. They show how much you've endured and survived. And they're sexy as hell."

He leaned forward and trailed his tongue over one such scar on her inner thigh. Allira hissed and squirmed under his kisses as he closed in on her slick pussy, but never quite reaching it. He wanted to build up her arousal for his entrance.

You always did make an impressive entrance.

Words from his past damn near derailed him, but Allira whimpered again and he was brought back to the task at hand. Her scent beguiled him and made his cock stiffen enough to bring a little pain. He'd wanted her for days, and always had to walk away. But tonight, he wasn't walking.

He stroked his fingers from her ankles to her knees, drawing them over his shoulders before settling his chest against the bed. Rich musk hit his nose and made his mouth water. Pink petals of her woman's flower beckoned him with her slick dew, and he didn't bother to wait longer.

His first taste of her exploded across his senses, honey with a hint of peach, and he dove in for more. He slid his tongue between her inner petals, lapping up the sweet juices flowing from her slit. Each swipe of his tongue made her moan, especially when he brushed the hood of her clitoris.

"Sweet glory. Do that again."

He was happy to comply, and settled his mouth over her clit to suck on it in earnest. Allira bucked her hips, grinding against his face to get closer, offering her succulent honey. Josten dove in like a king at feast—one of the few times he accepted being royalty these days.

He lapped at her petals, enjoying the slick texture against his tongue as he slid his hands between her thighs and opened her labia wider. She writhed under his ministrations as he dipped his head lower to probe her slit with his tongue. The honey and peach flavor intensified, and he moaned against her sensitive flesh as it flooded his mouth.

She answered with her own moan as he pressed a finger into her entrance, tickling the edges with the tip. She whined and wiggled her hips, but he held her still with his other hand and pushed his finger into her clenching sheath. She let out a sigh as if that was what she'd wanted from the beginning, and he swallowed a chuckle.

It's what I've wanted for a while, too.

His cock gave a hearty flex in agreement, and he promised himself he'd be seated in her slick warmth soon.

He started a rhythm with his finger and synced with licking her folds until Allira was rocking against his face in time with his strokes. Her sweet juices soaked his hand and his chin as he sucked on her clit. Even her sounds became more urgent and needy as her hips sped up, and he increased the frequency of his strokes.

When he sucked hard on her clit and added a second finger, Allira clamped down on his hand and wailed her ecstasy, throwing her head back. She shuddered with her release as he kept sucking and stroking until her body slowly relaxed into the bed. A flush of pleasure rippled down her body, making her cheeks, belly and breasts glow rosy in the lantern light.

Josten sat back and sucked her sweetness off his fingers before wiping his mouth. He'd never seen anyone enjoy an orgasm so much. It was beautiful. *She* was beautiful, and his cock flexed again, with emphatic agreement. She was glorious, and he needed to feel her release against his shaft.

"Oh, Joss, that was..." Allira took a deep breath. "Glorious."

He chuckled as pride sparked in his chest. "I'm so glad you enjoyed, my lady. But I'm not done giving you pleasure yet. Perhaps I can interest you in a ride?" He crawled onto the bed and braced himself on hands and knees over her.

She tilted her head, her hair fanned across the pillows. "A ride?"

"Yes." He lowered his hips and let the tip of his stiff cock brush against the wet curls on her vulva. "I've found a good, hard ride always relaxes me." He added a little more pressure and rubbed his cockhead into her moist labia.

"Ooh, I see. You *are* looking a little stiff. Do you need me to help you with that?" She sat up and scooted to the side so he could take her place on the bed.

"If you're so inclined, yes, please." He grinned as he settled on his back, his shaft bouncing stiffly against his belly.

"Oh, I'm inclined. In fact, I'm determined." She rolled onto her knees and grasped his cock, licking her lips as she watched the pre-cum bead at the slit. "This looks delicious. As much as I want to ride, I also want to taste."

It was a good thing Josten gasped because when Allira's hot mouth closed around his cockhead, he stopped breathing. The wet heat surrounding his cock made his eyes roll back in his head, and he saw stars. He wanted to fist her hair and help her get the right rhythm, but he forced his hands to clench the bedsheets instead. Better to let her find the pattern before he directed anything.

She settled into soft, nibbling kisses along his shaft down to his balls, where she kissed the sensitive skin between his thighs. He found himself moaning at her soft touches, and wondered why he'd never enjoyed such teasing strokes before.

Because you were always just trying to get off.

That was true, and this was different. He didn't want to just get off. He wanted to enjoy her company and her ministrations. He wanted the build-up of pleasure and emotional connection, where she took pleasure from him and he took pleasure from her. A mutual sharing and a deepening of their relationship.

When she raked her teeth over the edge of his glans, he gasped and rocked his hips, shoving his cock deeper into her hot mouth. She closed her lips around his flesh and slid her tongue on the shaft, sending bright sparks of arousal straight up his spine.

"Oh, fuck, Allira, that feels so damn good. Suck my cock, bright star." He had no idea where the endearment came from, but it fit her and sounded so right to him that he didn't question.

She moaned against his shaft and pulled back before licking the head and sliding back down. She repeated the motion in a steady rhythm, and his arousal built with inexorable advancement. But the moment that pushed him almost to the brink was when she cupped his balls with her free hand and the tips of her breasts brushed his hip.

He almost lost control on his release, but he gritted his teeth and grasped her head with his hands.

"Enough, bright star. I want to be inside you. Come ride me like you promised."

At first, disappointment flashed across her expression, but when she met his gaze, she smirked at the barely held-back strain she read on his face. She straddled his hips, trapping his wet cock between them, and leaned forward to kiss him. He could still smell her honey and peach scent along with his muskier flavor on her lips as she plundered his mouth with her tongue.

Intense pleasure made his cock try to flex, but it was trapped between their bodies. Despite its immobility, Allira giggled as she sat up, reaching between her legs to squeeze him.

"I'm getting the message that you want more than just kisses."

"Oh, you have no idea."

He helped steady her as she knelt up and grabbed his cock, fitting it to her entrance.

"Are you ready, Joss?"

He shivered in anticipation. "Ride me, Allira."

She grinned as she let herself slide down on his shaft. They both groaned as he came to rest, balls-deep, inside her tight channel. Hot, slick pressure engulfed him, and he closed his eyes to savor the feeling of her around him.

This has to be what bliss feels like.

Then she moved.

At first, he wasn't ready and wished she'd let him enjoy her tight sheath a little longer. But as she rocked up and down on his shaft with a gentle undulation of her hips, her clit scraped the head of his cock, and a new sensation built his arousal again.

"Sweet glory, Josten. That feels so damn good."

He agreed though he didn't have the concentration to respond as she increased the speed of her undulations. The friction built up between them, sending pleasure surging through his body and increasing his arousal. He grasped her hips and rocked his, meeting her thrusts as the heat of their coupling increased.

His orgasm built but there was no way he'd go over the precipice alone. He gritted his teeth and focused his gaze on the woman grinding on his cock. Her breasts bounced with each thrust and her skin flushed in the rosy glow he'd seen before. Everything about her was beautiful, from her taut nipples to the wet curls engulfing his shaft. His heart swelled in his chest, and he growled his approval.

"That's it, Allira. Take all of my cock. Fuck me hard. Yes." He thrust his hips harder, hoping his cock stroked her clit with every slide of his body into hers.

"Oh glory, Josten. I'm gonna come."

Her sheath tightened around his cock in a crushing grip and his release slipped its leash, crashing through him. He roared his jubilation as his mind flew into the cosmos filled with soft clouds, comfort, and acceptance. It was a place where everything was right in his world, and he never wanted to leave.

This is what I've been searching for through all of my existence.

The thought jarred him back to the present and he opened his eyes. For a moment, he couldn't quite understand what he was seeing. Where were the lanterns and the soft room with the bed? Where was Allira? He turned his head and scanned the room. All that greeted him was the waterfall and the soft glow of the lume worms around the catch pool.

Dreck and scars, was that a dream?

He leaned forward and rested his head in his hands as he thought over the memories of his time with Allira. It was all a dream—he didn't know he could still do that—but he didn't want it to remain that way. He scrubbed his face with his hands as he caught his breath.

The story of The Curse of the Rusty Crown insinuated that he had to atone for the wrongs he'd committed, and he was finally ready to see the real value of life were people and the experiences he had with them. It wasn't power, or coins, or control, or land. It was spending time with loved ones and connecting with others as a family and community.

He had no idea what all he'd need to do to atone for the wrongs he'd committed when a young and stupid, power-hungry idiot, but he'd do everything in his power to make amends. He wanted time with Allira. He wanted a future, and the only way to do that was to be a better being than he'd been in life.

And you have to tell her who and what you are.

Yeah, and that. The problem was, he had no idea how.

Chapter Twelve

S *weet glory!*

Allira scrubbed her face with her hands as she sat up in her bedroll. She felt out of breath though she'd been sound asleep. But her dreams. Woo-whee, that had been a hot dream. She hadn't had one of those since she was a teenager and the cute neighbor had smiled at her on market day. Of course, Josten was sexier and older than the neighbor, and she'd gotten much more enjoyment out of her dream this time around.

She took a few deep breaths to gather her awareness in the present rather than in her sexy dream, but she was loathe to let it go. It was everything she really wanted—a home near the Dreadstone Tombs and Josten. It had been perfect.

At least I now know what I truly want.

Shaking away the remnants of their hot and heavy tryst, she rose and revved up the fire before heading out to feed the horses. The day started out gloomy, with fog creeping through the trees, giving the Tombs a more sinister feel. She wrapped her cloak around her shoulders and made tea, shivering against the damp, cool temperatures.

She'd stopped going to the clearing in front of the Tombs' gates, but her gut said something would happen that day.

Maybe the idiots will all get killed off and we can call it done.

By her count, there were six knights left, including Markus Swindell. That was one guy she wouldn't mind never seeing again. He gave her the creeps, and he hadn't improved in the few weeks she'd been with the festival knights. She doubted he had many friends in the camp.

She snorted at her own thought.

This is a competition, not an expedition. Friends are a liability.

She laid more wood on the fire and wondered when Josten would appear as she sipped her tea and ate a cold breakfast of dried meat and leftover tubers. Memories of the dream heated her cheeks, and she was glad he wasn't there to see her blush.

The day lightened as the sun rose, but the fog persisted and she shivered in her cloak despite the fire. She added another log to the flames and glanced around her camp. If she decided to stay longer, it might make some sense to build another wall to her small sleeping kiosk to keep the weather out should the wind shift directions.

She laughed aloud.

"Here I am thinking about making permanent plans after a couple of weeks."

"Do you always talk to yourself in the fog?"

Josten's voice made her whirl, and she pressed her hand to her chest to keep her heart from leaping out of it.

"Sweet glory, warn a woman when you sift out of the fog, willya?" She shook her head. "No, I only talk to myself when I think something so outrageous it has to be spoken aloud so I can hear the ridiculousness of it."

He tilted his head and his long hair brushed the fur-covered shoulders of his cloak. "Is it ridiculous? I can see you building a platform around the fire pit to sit on with chairs and potted plants."

She blinked as he described the vision out of her dream. "You can?"

He nodded. "Of course, you could move the fire pit out a bit and expand on the structure to make a true dwelling, then build the sitting platform from that. The Orcs and Goblins could help."

"You seem pretty sure they'd be fine with me staying." She finished her tea and set the mug down. "Do you want some tea? It's damp out here."

He shook his head. "I'm good. And I *know* they'll be fine with it, especially if I put in a good word for you." He paused a moment, his gaze focused on the fire before he swung it back to hers. "I'd like you to stay if it's something you think you'd prefer. Your company has been a bright spot in my life for I don't know how long."

She couldn't help her giddy smile. "Thanks for that. It's the same for me." Then she finished her tea and set the cup aside. "I feel like going for a walk. You interested in joining me?"

"I'd be delighted." He grinned and gestured for her to precede him.

"Such a gentleman."

She tightened her cloak around her and took a deep breath of the damp air. While it wasn't her favorite weather, she liked being bundled up and warm with good company.

I could totally get used to this.

They headed through the trees toward the clearing in front of the gate to the Tombs, and she realized she already had made her decision to stay. She was done being a mercenary, and she definitely didn't want to be a farmer—despite the garden she had planned. What would her life be like if she stayed in the shadow of the Tombs?

Quieter.

But not necessarily lonely. She could trade with the Goblins and Orcs, though she wasn't sure what she'd trade, and live small with her horses. And perhaps with a little company. She glanced over at Josten, and it reminded her of her dream.

She'd definitely welcome *that* kind of company.

She was about to tell Josten she'd like him to ask Mectarn for permission to stay when they stepped through the misty trees into the clearing. Everything seemed calm and normal, but unease slithered down her spine as she took in the four horses waiting in the shadow of the trees.

She recognized the crests of Swindell, Barnsworth, Hornsby, and Craven on the saddles, and Craven's brown and white paint. The world was almost breathless—no wind rustled the trees and the mist crept between the trunks like ghosts. Still, the hairs at her nape stood up, and she stepped backwards into the shadow of the trees, waiting for the other shoe to drop.

As if on cue, screams filled the clearing, making the horses jerk their heads up and spook. Allira jumped and shot a look toward the gate. Figures boiled out of the entrance, men in armor running hell-bent-for-leather toward the horses. Behind them came furious Orcs, their amber eyes damn near glowing with fury in the faded light.

Swindell was ahead of two of the other men, and he slashed the picket line with his sword before leaping onto his mount. He swung his gaze to look behind him and stopped when he saw her in the trees. An ugly snarl curled his lips before he spurred away, leaving the others to catch their horses. Barnsworth limped, but he made it to his horse despite the blood running down his right arm and left leg. He struggled to mount his panicked ride, but finally lurched into the saddle and rode away.

Craven, however, screamed at the other two to wait as he hobbled toward his spooked paint. But an arrow caught him in the back, throwing him to the ground. He cried out and started crawling, desperate to get away, but the Orcs caught up to him. No one said anything more than growls, and the biggest of the lot unhooked a huge battleax and brought one side of the double blade down across Craven's neck. The man stopped making noise and moving.

Allira swallowed hard, hoping the Orcs wouldn't hate her as much as those who'd caused weeks' worth of damage.

She looked around for Josten, but he'd left her side without a word. She found him beside the big Orc, and he stiffened from whatever the gren had to say.

"Allira!"

She jumped again and took a deep breath before hurrying to Josten's side, hoping that the gren wouldn't cleave her skull from her shoulders.

"What's going on?"

"I need to go to help the gren and grells—the fucking monsters attacked the village."

"What?" She gaped. "The village? But there's no treasure in the village, right? I mean, nothing that's the rumored piles of gold. Why would they do this?"

"They're monsters," Josten said flatly. "And there is a little bit of gold, but not enough to merit this kind of destruction."

There was nothing to say to that, and she glanced down at the decapitated man on the ground. "I'll stay out here and help clean up this mess. It looks like I get another two horses, anyway."

"Leave the horses. Help me patch up the injured and repair the village." He pointed toward the Tombs.

Allira swallowed hard as she shot a look at the gren standing beside them. "Are you sure? I mean, I didn't do this, but I'm a knight and human. I'm probably the last person they want to see in their village."

"Are you afraid to help, Allira?" His snapped question made her scowl.

"No, but I'm thinking of the people who just had a human attack them. Bringing me into their home might be an added stress they really don't need right now."

His expression lightened a little. "At this moment, they need help more than anything. If you want to stay nearby, it would be good to pitch in for your neighbors."

She couldn't argue with that so she nodded and followed Josten into the Tombs. Some of the gren and grells gave her wary looks, but she hadn't brought more than her dagger, and she dipped her chin to them as she passed. She straightened her shoulders and walked like she was supposed to be there, a neighbor willing to help. She just hoped they saw her that way.

She expected them to enter the way the knights came out, but to her surprise, Josten led her farther around the eastern edge of the bluffs on a trail she'd assumed was made by animals. But the trail ended at a crevice not much wider than Josten's shoulders. There were guards waiting a few paces inside the small entrance, and lanterns sat on evenly spaced shelves along the passage to give light.

The corridor was well kept and free of debris, and only traveled about fifty yards before they passed through an arched doorway into a larger space.

Allira gasped.

Cliff dwellings made from perfectly cut bricks and small stones constructed a large and intricate village with homes of various sizes filling the cave. She'd seen books in the book shops with drawings of places like this, but they were always abandoned, at least according to the authors. But this was a living, breathing community.

Now, some of the houses were broken, trailing lines of earthen bricks, with splotches of blood staining their rough sides. Lanterns had been lit to give more light, but there were a few holes in the ceiling of the cave to allow the dim, foggy light of day to hit the floor. Nothing disguised the damage the human knights had done to the people and dwellings.

"Sweet glory." Allira took in the broken homes and focused on the injured Goblins and Orcs milling about. "Josten, I don't know if this is a good idea."

"They need to know you're not like the invaders. They need to know you're willing to help."

"I don't think they'll believe I'm here to help." She waved at the broken houses. "Even with your endorsement, they're going to think I'm here to finish the job."

"Then we show them you're a friend not an enemy."

Josten headed straight into the portion of the village with the most damage, and Allira followed close behind him, hoping no one would see her as a threat. A few of the Orcs stiffened when she came near, but the Goblins seemed to accept her because Josten stood beside her.

She let her gaze slide around the cavern and found three Orcs carrying another body, this one still in its armor. Hornsby. The corpse was missing a few key limbs, but must have bled out elsewhere because it wasn't leaking bodily fluids. Allira couldn't feel anything but disgust for the asshole and turned her attention back to Josten's discussion with the grells.

It took a few minutes to ask what the people needed, but as soon as Allira had an idea, she immediately got to work on moving the debris out of the way and stacking the bricks neatly to the side. Gundri eventually found her, and they worked together to make it easier for the masons to repair the homes destroyed. Some of Allira's tension fled when Gundri gave her an encouraging smile.

"Thank you for doing this, Allira-dri." Gundri straightened and brushed the grit off her hands. "It's kind of you."

"You're welcome. I want to help. You folks are good neighbors, and I like my little camp beside the Tombs."

Gundri raised her eyebrows. "Even when your nearest neighbors are Goblins, Orcs, and Nagas?"

Allira nodded. "Better people than the humans any day."

"Swikar to that."

"Swikar?"

"It's a way of emphatically agreeing with someone in our home language." Gundri stretched her back. "Come, let's go help prepare some food for the other workers."

"Sounds great. Were many of your people hurt?"

"A fair few, but we drove off those monsters before they did too much damage—"

"Allira!"

She jumped as Josten's voice cracked like a whip, and turned to look at him, afraid he was going to tell her to get lost once and for all. To her surprise, Gundri straightened and stood shoulder-to-shoulder with her, squaring off with Josten's approach in a show of support.

"What is it, Josten?" She saw Gundri jerk in surprise out of the corner of her eye, but she kept her gaze on the man.

"No one has seen Mectarn, and we think she's injured. I need you to come with me to find her."

She blinked and glanced at Gundri. "Are you sure? Mectarn is your shaman, right? Do you really want a human on the search team? I don't want to overstep."

"How do you know Mada Mectarn is injured, Highness?" Gundri's voice came out as a whisper.

"I can feel it." Josten glanced at her a moment. "Would you come with us, Gundri? We'll need at least two to carry Mada Mectarn if she can't walk back to the village."

"Of course, Highness. And I can speak for Allira if anyone asks why there's a human in the Tombs." Gundri inclined her head, the beads at the ends of her braids clacking together.

"Good." Josten nodded sharply. "We'll need torches. How are your tracking abilities, Allira?"

She shrugged. "I'm above average at it."

For just a moment, his expression softened into a humorous smile. "Above average? Is that your way of saying you're pretty good at it?" He handed her a torch.

"They didn't make me a scout in my early days for nothin'." She shot him her best cocksure smirk then glanced around at the village and the myriads of footprints. "Where are we starting?"

Josten closed his eyes, and the edges of him wavered, like he had no form or substance. Allira frowned and almost reached for him, but Gundri didn't seem alarmed so she kept her unease quiet.

When he opened his eyes, he pointed to the back of the village. "Let's start there."

Allira and Gundri, along with another Goblin and Orc, followed Josten to the edge of the village where a corridor led deeper into the Tombs. From the smell wafting out of it, Allira surmised there was a river or hot springs behind the stone walls.

Allira lifted the torch and scanned the tunnel. Scuffed footprints filled the dirt path, and splattered blood marked the walls. She couldn't tell if it was human or Goblin blood because of the shifting light, but someone had been injured enough to leave a trail. After careful examination, she found blood drops farther on. Followed by large, booted prints.

"They went this way, and someone was injured. See the blood drops? They have little streaks in the direction of movement." She moved the flaming torch close to the floor.

"It smells like Goblin blood." Gundri's expression hardened. "It smells like Mada Mectarn."

"Let's follow and see how far it goes."

Allira carefully stepped around the blood trail, keeping her gaze trained on the ground. She periodically looked up to see if there were any details on the walls, but she kept looking for signs of struggle.

When the corridor opened up enough for four men to walk abreast, she found it.

She knelt on the floor, studying the footprints and the trail of dark green blood, black in the torchlight. From the drag marks, she could tell Mectarn's left leg was injured in the assault and wasn't functioning as it should. She glanced up. A splotch of green blood marred the edge of the cave's wall.

"What can you see?" Josten's voice echoed strangely in the cavern—almost hollow like death itself. "Did Mectarn get away?"

"Looks like someone wounded her and she fell here." Allira pointed to the impression of a knee in the dirt. "From there, it's hard to tell if this is where—"

"She fell?" Gundri took a few steps down the corridor and swung her gaze around. "I don't see her anywhere."

"I think she managed to get away." Allira pointed deeper into the maze of passages. "Where does this go?"

"Toward the hot springs that are used for healing and laundry cleaning."

Allira rose to her feet and shot them a look of surprise. "Goblins do laundry?"

Josten scowled. "Of course they do laundry. Everyone does. How do you think they keep their homes free from blood and viscera?"

"Yeah, that doesn't improve my impression." She shook her head as Gundri smirked and moved off in the direction of the blood trail. "When we find Mectarn, are there others who can help her heal?"

"Though she's the medicine woman of our clan, she has apprentices. She sees to the welfare of the whole clan as well as helps the other women in birth and medical care." Gundri followed with Josten behind, her voice barely louder than a whisper. "Not that the rest of us aren't as important, but she helps everyone, including the invaders."

Allira paused and shot her a surprised look. "You mean, she helps to heal the idiots who invade her home?"

Josten nodded while Gundri shrugged. "It's her way."

Allira scowled. "Fucking bastards. This needs to be the last time they do this. None of you ask to be attacked each year."

"Nope, but humans don't see us as people. Just monsters."

"The only monsters here are the humans invading."

Gundri nodded. "Won't argue with that."

Josten pushed past them, but stopped in the corridor. Several doorways led to various passageways and rooms off the main corridor, and he glanced helplessly around.

"I've lost the sense of her."

Allira studied the door where steam billowed out. "I think she went in there. Do you see the drag marks of her injured foot?" She pointed at a dark doorway.

"That's the soak baths." Gundri bit her lip. "It would make a decent place to hide."

"Give me a second."

Allira stepped in to a room full of steam and lume worms glowing from the ceiling. She scanned the space, looking for blood and footprints. The blood was obscured by the steam, but deep footprints marred the floor near the entrance cave. Using the torch, she frowned. She expected the prints from the knights' boots to be all over the muddy, slick ground, but she found nothing.

She spun and backtracked, starting from the entrance again.

"It looks like only Mectarn came in here. The humans never made it past the entrance."

"Mectarn! We're here to help. Tell us where you are!" Josten's voice filled the whole room and made all the Orcs tighten their hands on their weapons.

Everyone held their breath, listening to hear a response. Allira held the torch aloft and bit her lip, hoping she'd led the Goblins where their shaman hid.

"I'm here."

The voice was so soft it blended with the sounds of bubbling water at first, and Allira wasn't sure if she actually heard words or if it was just her hope. After a few moments, she heard it again.

"I'm here, Highness."

Gundri was already moving as Allira held the torch up higher. The Orcs surged after Gundri, and they found Mectarn wedged into a small alcove out of sight of the doorway. Allira clenched her jaw tight against the damage on the woman's face and body. One arm lay swollen across her waist while the other gripped a short bone dagger. Her face sported one black eye and a split lip. And her left leg wouldn't fold like it was supposed to.

Those bastards deserved everything they got.

"Oh, Mada Mectarn, I'm so sorry we failed you." Gundri's eyes filled with tears, but her motions were sure and gentle.

"It is...not your responsibility." Mectarn tried to give her a smile, but the gren jostled her and she whimpered.

"Be careful. She's fragile right now." Josten directed the gren carry Mectarn back to the village as Allira stepped out of the way, chagrin filling her soul.

There's no way they're going to agree to let me stay after this.

Since she had the only light source, she took the lead back to the village, trying not to get in anyone's way or meet anyone's gaze straight on. The other denizens of the Tombs watched her warily, but no one outright said she should leave.

Gundri went ahead to one of the unbroken dwellings and lit the lanterns inside, before commandeering other grells to help her set up a comfortable place for Mectarn to rest. Allira stood back as Josten stepped inside and spoke with the injured Medicine Woman for a short time. She wondered if they were discussing what should be done with the one human knight who'd come with the invaders, but hadn't actually participated in the destruction.

One of two options—kill me and use my body for fertilizer, or chase me all the way back to Capstone Creek.

Allira glanced around and wondered if she'd be able to leave. She didn't want to intrude on the village's healing, and she was definitely the outsider. Gundri left the stone house where they'd installed Mectarn, but seemed to be on a mission and never looked at Allira.

She bit her lip and glanced around for the exit. The lit corridor heading back toward the secret entrance reminded her of her grandmothers' home at night with the flickering candles, beckoning warmth and safety. This time, the torches offered escape.

But before she could take more than a couple of steps, Josten reappeared and looked for her.

"Allira."

She stopped and glanced back at him. "Yes?"

"Mectarn is asking for you."

She blinked. "Me? Why?"

He just raised an eyebrow, and she swallowed hard before reversing her steps and following him into the unbroken house.

Despite its somewhat primitive shape, the house had colorful cushions and wooden furniture to make it more comfortable. The injured shaman lay on a pallet with brightly woven blankets and pillows that looked soft. Her hair had been braided into neat rows with beads and feathers woven into them. They were long enough to reach her breasts, but were stained green with her blood. Bruises and swelling marred her face, but her pale gold eyes showed awareness and depth.

"Ah, you...must be...Allira-dri." Mectarn's voice came in halting breaths, suggesting her ribs had been broken.

"I am." Allira bowed her head in respect.

"I understand...you led...my people to...me...Thank you."

"It was the least I could do. Your people have been very kind and gracious with my presence near your home. I..." Allira grimaced and shook her head. "I regret my part in the humans' arrival here. From now on, I'll do my best to stop this tradition from continuing."

The shaman gazed at her for so long she wondered if the grell would tell her to take a flying leap. Her spirits sank lower and lower until she resisted the urge to fidget in discomfort.

"I believe you."

Allira damn near wilted in relief but she nodded. "Thank you."

"You...came with...them, but...you chose...not to...enter our caves...Why?"

She shot a look at Josten before returning her gaze to Mectarn. "At first, it was because I didn't want to be here—I was coerced. But after I met Josten and the other grells and gren, I realized the knights were committing raids and murder to gain glory. They didn't see you as people, and I couldn't see you as anything but people."

"Even...if we...are Goblins...your monsters?" Mectarn raised an eyebrow.

"The only monsters in the Tombs are the humans. Your people live here—it's your home and we're the intruders. I'm not with those men. I don't believe in what they're doing, but I also recognize it's not that simple because of what I am. I'm one of the monsters harming your village. And I'm very sorry."

"You are...not to...blame, Allira Maplestaff...You...have treated...our people...with honor and...respect." Mectarn shifted and grimaced. "You have...not done...this."

"No, but I didn't do enough to stop it." She rested one hand on Mectarn's. "I will try to stop it from now on."

Mectarn grunted and turned her gaze to Josten as Allira released her.

"I...should've...taken your suggestion...Highness." Mectarn's words stretched with her breaths. "I'm...sorry."

Josten shook his head. "My suggestion?"

The shaman nodded. "To fortify...the village's...defenses. I thought...we were...too far... from the...treasure for...their interest. I was...wrong."

He held up his hand. "Don't apologize. Use your energy to heal. Is there anything more we can do for you?"

The Medicine Woman grew thoughtful, her gaze sliding over to Allira. "You...said she's the...warrior...who seeks...to be our...neighbor, Highness?"

Josten raised his eyebrows. "She is."

Allira grimaced. "Uh, well, I was thinking about it. But after today's carnage, I'm uncertain of my welcome."

Mectarn narrowed her eyes. "Were you...the one...to help clean up...the debris...before?"

Allira nodded. "Yes. Gundri called me the Dismemberer of Dreadstone. I used the broken bits of gear to decorate my camp. It turned out surprisingly festive."

Mectarn grunted with amusement. "Fitting. You were...a member...of their party, though?"

Allira took a deep breath. "I came with them, conscripted to be their thirteenth warrior, but I had no interest in treasure or raiding. I came only because it guarantees my grandmothers' prosperity."

Mectarn winced as she tried to find a comfortable position. "And yet...you wish to stay...near the Tombs...as you call them? Despite their inhabitants?"

Allira shot a look at Josten before she nodded. "Yes, I do."

"Why?"

"I like it here. Your forest is beautiful and calm. I'm content here for the first time in my life." She shot another look at Josten. "And the company has been good."

"Oh-ho, it's more...than land that holds...your interest, is it?" Mectarn nodded, a little smirk creasing her lips. "I'm grateful...for your help and...your willingness to defend...my people. I will think on...your request. But now...I must rest."

Josten bowed and backed way. "Be well. We'll check on you later."

The grell nodded and closed her eyes, and Allira followed Josten out of the house to stand in the village square. Neither of them said anything for a few moments, and Allira wondered if he would decide he never wanted to see her again. Why would he? The other members of her 'party' had destroyed the people he cared for most in the world.

"I'm really sorry, Josten." She reached out to him, but he stepped aside so her hand missed. She pulled it back and held her elbows as she glanced around. "Maybe I should go back to my camp. I still need to collect the horses."

"Oh, right. Of course." He gestured toward another corridor opposite the way they'd come in from the secret entrance. "This is the fastest way to get to the front entrance."

He led her through the winding and twisting passage with blind turns and corners, and she wondered how the hell Swindell and the others had figured out the way to the village when it seemed like endless dead ends.

Why would they even come this way?

There was no light or sounds filtering from the village at the other end of the branching tunnel. Why would the knights take this dark passage?

A horrible thought occurred to Allira. Were the knights *chasing* escaping Goblins and Orcs?

Allira's gut sank. If Swindell chased the Goblins back to their home, it meant he'd lost track of what he was supposed to be doing. Why hunt the defenders if they were running away? Wasn't the point to clear them from the spaces so the knights could loot?

Sweet glory, if he's hunting the denizens of the Tombs, he's totally lost his mind.

She stumbled and caught herself on the wall as she considered if Swindell had suffered some sort of mental break. That would make him far more dangerous than he'd been before. She swallowed hard and shoved the thought away. She couldn't prove it, and it wouldn't help to voice her concerns.

"Are you all right, Allira?" Josten looked back with distracted concern as they stepped into a wider corridor.

"Yeah, I'm okay. What about you? How are you holding up?"

He grimaced. "I'm worried about Mectarn. Her energy is weak, and any little thing could shift it toward death." His jaw tightened. "We can't lose her. She's the glue that holds this community together with wisdom and strength."

"Do you think she'll pull through?" Allira nodded to the Goblins she passed and several nodded back, but a few snarled at her with distrust.

"I don't know. Letting her rest is all we can do."

They continued on through the Tombs, passing another pile of discarded armor and weapons covered in orc blood. Allira paused to see if she could find another broken blade to match the first one she'd collected. She didn't see anything that would suit so she hurried after Josten toward the archway leading to the main cave.

The entrance room was a huge hall with sculpted columns carved from white veined rock and a floor made of smooth flagstones. It looked like the main halls from any number of famous castles and fortresses she'd seen over the years, but instead of a dais with a throne at the end, it merely had a stepped platform that led to other rooms. Doorways and broken balustrades decorated the walls of the room, and the floor now held debris the size of small ponies littering the space.

They make great obstacles to deter invaders.

Not that it had stopped the men like Swindell, Barnsworth, Hornsby, and Craven from nearly killing Mectarn. Fury rose in Allira's chest. It was unacceptable that these men could come in and kill the residents who had occupied the Tombs since the Dreadstone King had died. They were *people*. The humans were the monsters.

Maybe if the king was still around, this bloody tradition would end.

She shot a look at Josten as he paused in front of the stepped platform, his arms crossed over his red, riveted doublet, and for a moment, she could picture him wearing a crown and presiding over everyone in the hall.

Like a king—the Dreadstone King.

She stumbled again as Mectarn's address of Josten flashed through her mind. She'd called him 'Highness,' like he had a position of royalty among the denizens of the Tombs. Allira narrowed her eyes as she took in Josten's form and clothing.

Yeah, some of his clothes were out-of-date, more typical of the warrior kings from centuries past with his deep-red quilted, pinned doublet and matching bracers in leather, the chainmail shirt, and the fur-shouldered woolen cloak he only wore when visiting outside the Tombs. His boots were mid-calf and flat-soled with differentiated toes.

Most of the knights she'd come with wore longer leather doublets and long-sleeved mail shirts. Their boots were knee-height and square-toed with heels. While their dress wasn't terribly different from Josten's, he definitely wore the older styles.

And never seems to change them, but doesn't stink with bad body funk.

"Josten, why did Mectarn call you 'highness'?"

He switched his gaze to her and uncrossed his arms before moving toward the entrance to the Tombs. His shoulders tightened, and his hands closed into loose fists as he strode ahead of her.

"Did she? I didn't notice." Despite his words, his voice sounded overly casual.

"Do you hold some sort of title or position in the Tombs that I'm not aware of?" She hurried to catch up to him to try to read his expression, but he glanced away as if looking for listeners. "I noticed that the gren and grells all defer to you, and do as you ask."

"It's more of an honorary thing because I've been around a long time." He still kept his expression closed down.

"How long have you lived around here?" She reached out for his shoulder, but he saw her and dodged at the last moment as they exited the Tombs. "Hey, slow down, I'm not going to goose you or anything."

He had the grace to look chagrinned as they stepped into the blustery day. They found Craven's paint and Hornsby's chestnut where they'd left them. Someone had come and taken Craven's body and disposed of it.

Good riddance to bad rubbish.

Josten ran his hands through his hair. "Sorry. My mind was on what we could gather to help Mectarn recover."

"Yeah, I'm worried about her, too. I don't think there's anything we can do but hope she's strong enough." Allira headed for the drowsing horses. "I'll take the horses home with the others, unless you want one? The mare's a pretty good horse from what I've seen."

"No, I don't need horses at the moment. You take her."

Allira nodded. "Okay. I'll add these two to the herd. Goddess knows, I have the space."

"Do you have enough feed for them? Your herd's quite large now." Josten stood back as she tightened the girths on the saddles to keep them from sliding off the mounts.

Allira frowned a bit. "I don't know. I'll have to check." She released the horses from the trees to which they'd been tied, turning for camp. The Goblins must have caught them and secured them after Swindell's and Barnsworth's departure.

"Let me come with you. If you need some, I can let the gren and grells know." He fell in beside her as she headed for camp.

"Are you sure they're still good with helping me? I mean, the other humans just gravely wounded their shaman. I know she doesn't blame me, but at the moment, she can't speak for me. Are you sure the others won't write me off as another threat?"

Josten shook his head. "They don't see you as one of the knights anymore, especially Gundri, and many of the others listen to her. You've been kind and friendly, willing to see them as full sentient people rather than monsters. It sets you apart."

She sighed and patted Craven's mare, her presence a reminder of the death the knights had wrought. "Speaking of monsters, since you live around here, did you ever meet the Dreadstone King?"

Josten stiffened then shot her a sidelong glance. "The Dreadstone King, Demon of the Deeps, Killer of Heroes, and Keeper of the Secrets? That Dreadstone King?"

"Wow, I had no idea he had so many names." She narrowed her eyes. "But yes, that Dreadstone King."

"Not recently."

Allira raised her eyebrows. "But you *have* met him?"

Josten nodded, the edges of his mouth pulling down. "A long time ago."

She watched him a few moments, trying to gauge what he *wasn't* saying. "The last reports of the Dreadstone King were over seventy years ago." She pointedly looked him up and down. "You're not that old... Are you?"

He sighed and looked away as they came through the trees to her camp. The two new horses whinnied to the others in the corral, and they answered. Allira laughed at the antics, but she kept her attention on Josten as he walked with them to the corral.

"Would you get the gate for me? I'm going to take off their tack." Allira tied the horses to the fence and shifted to the mare's saddle to begin removing it.

"Uh, yes, right."

She'd never heard Josten so uncertain before as he strode to the gate. He simply stared at the latch with intensity for a few moments before reaching out to lift the rope over the gate post. For a moment, it appeared he struggled, but the rope lifted and the gate swung free. Allira lifted the saddle off the horse and loosened the reins from the fence before leading her into the corral.

"All right, honey, you're free to go." She lifted the bridle over the mare's ears and set her free to visit with her herd mates.

She stepped back through to work on Hornsby's chestnut gelding. She focused on taking off the tack, but her mind churned over the puzzle of Josten. He still hadn't told her his surname, and every time she asked him about something personal, he looked panicked. She freed the gelding from his trappings and led him into the corral. She closed the gate and latched it before eyeing Josten.

"Hey, if you don't want to tell me anything, I don't really need answers. I just wondered how you seem to know so much about the Tombs and the Dreadstone King when you're just as human as me."

Josten sighed again but didn't say anything until Allira picked up the tack and took it to the increasing pile accumulating beside her tent in the lean-to. She frowned. She'd have to pack them up and send it all back to the families of the dead knights. Of course, she could deliver them herself when she returned to her family's farm.

If I return. Mectarn might agree to let me stay.

"It looks like you can use some feed for your horses. I'll be sure to tell the gren and grells about it when I get back to the Caverns." Josten's voice sounded strangely polite and official. "In the meantime, I'm going to help the others repair the village."

"Of course. Again, I'm really sorry this happened. It doesn't make any sense why the knights would go after the village." She scowled as she shook her head. "There wasn't any reason to go that way that I could see."

"No, there wasn't, but who knows what goes through the minds of monsters?"

Her shoulders dropped. "Yeah, you're right about that. Give my best to Gundri and the others, though I'm sure they'd rather see the back of me."

"Allira."

"Yes?"

Josten opened his mouth as if he wanted to say something but it stuck in his throat. After a moment or two, he shook his head. "I will send the grells to help with the horse feed after we've made progress on rebuilding the village."

"All right. Thanks, Josten."

He gave her a polite smile that didn't reach his eyes before he waved and disappeared into the trees.

Allira narrowed her eyes and wondered what he'd really meant to say.

Chapter Thirteen

Allira boiled some water and sat down with her brewed tea to watch the fading light over the corral as the sun sank. It had been a long and soggy day, and while the Goblins had come immediately after she'd gotten to camp to feed the horses, they'd been quiet and withdrawn. She'd thanked them and offered her sorrows for their losses, but they hadn't stayed to accept them. Her uncertainty about her welcome had eaten at her mood for the rest of the day, and she hadn't found the energy to do much more than ruminate all day.

I'm still ruminating now.

She frowned in thought as she sipped the brew. What the hell was up with Josten? He hadn't been back to see her since he'd left at midday, and that was unusual. She half expected him to come waltzing into camp for their usual bedtime story, but he hadn't showed. While she understood his concern for Mectarn and the village, she thought he'd come to see her one last time before bed.

It has something to do with the Dreadstone King.

Didn't all of this? The whole reason the knights came back to the Tombs, year after year, was the damn treasure rumored to have been collected by the king. She scowled and shook her head as she poured more tea. What a load of horseshit. The Tombs were called the Caverns and were inhabited. If there'd been any real treasure, it would've been found long ago.

She glanced down at the book she'd brought out to read. Maybe she could distract herself from Josten's odd reaction, but even the tome made her think of him. She picked it up and opened it to where she'd left off the day before, but the words didn't make sense and she couldn't concentrate.

Her mind kept flitting over to the odd conversation they'd had about the Dreadstone King and both Mectarn's and the other grens' and grells' address of him over the last fortnight. They all treated him as some sort of royalty. While she knew several of the knights who'd put in for the barbaric relic hunt were second or third children of aristocracy, no one ever deferred to them with the respect due a monarch.

But it would explain why the Goblins and Orcs helped me at his direction.

The question was, did they consider him the Dreadstone King? As far as the human records went, the man had died over seven decades ago, and hadn't been seen or heard from since. That was why there was a Festival of the Relic. The Relic was some magical artifact the king had owned, but he'd left no description of it, nor what magic it possessed.

Allira set aside her book and picked up her tea, staring meditatively into the fire.

Either someone originally knew what the Relic was and hadn't passed it on, or the story had been brought back to the human villages and exaggerated until it became riches, land, and power beyond one's wildest dreams granted by the Relic. Young fighters had swarmed at first, but year after year, no one claimed the prize or came back at all.

I wonder how the princess feels being another prize to be won this year.

Would she rejoice when no one came back alive or would she be disappointed?

Still, there was something about Josten's reaction after talking about the Dreadstone King that made Allira wonder what he knew. He wasn't old enough to have known the man, but perhaps he was the king's—much—younger nephew or cousin, which was why the Goblins deferred to him.

Allira drank her tea and let the thoughts chase themselves through her mind until it was time to make supper and feed the horses. Despite his abrupt departure, Josten must have told the gren to come back with more horse feed because she caught sight of Crent and Tral carrying large rolls of dried grasses for the animals. Allira waved, and relief settled in her gut at their respectful nods.

Maybe I still have honor as the Dismemberer of Dreadstone. She deposited her book on her bedroll and started supper.

She hoped Josten would return with news of Mectarn's progress, but the sun slid behind the cliffs and the light faded from the sky as she sat down to eat alone. She hadn't realized how much she'd counted on Josten's company at supper, even if he didn't eat.

Curious, that.

It hurt to think he was avoiding her, but maybe she couldn't really blame him. She'd arrived with the monsters attacking the people in the Caverns. She could be tainted by association.

And I'm human. But so is he... Right?

She shook her head and cleaned up her meal, before she banked the fire, and crawled into her tent. She wished she could understand what had set Josten off, but for the life of her, she couldn't determine what she'd said to make him retreat and stay away.

She settled down in her tent and watched the stars wheel overhead as her mind faded slowly into sleep. There'd be enough time to figure everything out in the morning. She let go and drifted off.

Someone hauled Allira bodily up from her sleeping roll by her shirt front, jerking her awake. Her mind snapped into focus on the crazed expression, the smells of rotting breath and old blood, and the hard, calloused hands dragging her from her tent. She automatically reached for the dagger she kept beside her bedroll, but her hand closed on nothing but air as she was thrown to the ground near her fire pit.

"You thought you were so smart, Maplestaff, moving closer to the Tombs. You think we wouldn't find you?" The guttural voice was damn near unrecognizable, but the light of the moon showed Markus Swindell's ravaged face scowling. "Was it really to keep a better eye on our horses—several of which are grazing in your corral—or was it because you're a fucking TRAITOR?" He roared the last as he lunged for her.

Allira had enough awareness to scramble away from him and onto her feet. Swindell was quick, though, and he grabbed her braided hair, yanking her back to him. Her own dagger magically appeared at her throat, held in his clenched fist, and his rancid, hot breath slithered into her ear.

"Are you looking for this? I found it next to your bed." He pressed it against her skin. "It's a good blade. Sharp and clean. I guess I can't fault you for your weapon care." He spun her around until she faced him with the point at her throat. "But I *can* fault you for abandoning your people and working *with* the monsters."

"What are you talking about, Swindell?" She inserted as much bewilderment into her voice as she could with her head twisted.

"I'm talking about *helping* the creatures that live in the Tombs! This is a nice camp you have. Did you build it all yourself, or were your new friends involved?" He yanked on her hair again. "Did they show you where the Relic is? Did they give you the key to the whole competition?"

"I've never been into the Tombs."

Okay, that wasn't strictly true. She'd gone inside when Josten asked her to help track Mectarn so they could find her. But she'd never gone looking for any treasure or the Relic.

"LIAR! I know you've been helping them. I saw you!" He shook her braid for emphasis.

Okay, fuck this.

She ducked her head and lunged forward, getting closer. She yanked her head up and slammed the back of her skull against his chin. Swindell yelped and released both her hair and her dagger. Allira dropped low and snagged the dagger before whirling away before he could grab her again. She expected him to drop after she clipped his chin, but his rage was such that he merely staggered and rubbed his face.

Well, hell.

She rose into a fighting crouch with the dagger held at the ready. That was the last time he'd catch her.

"Nice move. Didn't expect a coward like yourself to use it." His eyes glittered as he sized her up.

"What do you want, Swindell?"

"I want you to show me the way into the Tombs straight to the Relic. The prize is mine. I've *earned* it. I wasted days nursing those crybabies back to health. And what did they do? They fuckin' ran! Ran like the rabbits they were. Cowards, like you."

Allira held back a snort of derision. The last thing she needed to do was antagonize him. He'd already lost what sanity he had left, and she didn't need him enraged any more than he was.

"I can't show you the way. I've only gone in the main gate like you. Hell, you've probably seen more of the Tombs than I have."

Fuck!

She realized her admission too late, but she hoped he hadn't noticed her slip. Technically, she could try to convince him she'd only stepped inside the gate, and he *had* seen more of the Tombs—he'd spent days fighting and searching.

"So, you *have* been inside the Tombs. I knew it!" He stabbed a finger at her and shifted to the right, trying to get closer.

She moved in the exact opposite direction despite wearing no boots. She'd be damned if she let him touch her again.

"Just in the main gate, like I said."

She watched his movements. He was dressed for battle as if he'd gotten ready to storm the Tombs despite the sun having gone down. His sword wasn't in his grip, yet, but all his armor was strapped to his body and his weapons bristled around him. A few she recognized from some of the other knights.

What the fuck is he up to?

Had he planned to come here and accost her? What was his endgame? She shifted another step away from the crazed knight.

"I see you have a few new weapons. Is that Argyle's mace?" Allira took another step, hoping to get close to her sword.

"Yes, the stupid bastard died of his wounds. He took a pike to the gut." Swindell shrugged carelessly, but he took another step closer. "Don't worry, I only took the spoils of what was left. Just like you."

"What spoils do you mean?"

He scowled and waved at the horses curiously watching their tableau. "The warhorses."

"They were *left* behind. I didn't see any of you stop long enough to take them with you." She shook her head and moved closer to her tent. "They needed someone to care for them. I brought them here and built a corral to keep them safe."

She was almost there. All she had to do was dive into her tent and grab her sword, then she'd be on equal footing. Well, almost. She still needed her boots. She watched him as he clenched and unclenched his gauntleted hands, his sneer warping his normally handsome features.

This guy's completely off the deep end.

At last, he put the fire pit completely between them, and she dove into her tent for her sword. Except she couldn't find it. She scrabbled around in the bedding for it, but the only weapon she found were her boots.

"Looking for this?"

The smirk was clear in Swindell's voice even if she couldn't see his face. She *could* see the sharp edge of her own sword in his hand, pointing at her throat.

This is not the way I like being woken up.

"Oh, good. You found it. I was looking for that. May I have it, please?" She did her best to keep her voice dry and sarcastic so it wouldn't betray her mounting unease.

"No, I think I'll keep this for a while. Get up." He gestured with the tip.

"Why?"

"Because I'll run you through if you don't."

"Good point. Literally." She scooted closer to the entrance. "Can I put on my boots first?"

He hesitated as if he would deny her, but she tugged on the first one before he could say anything.

"I can't take you into the Tombs if I don't have my boots." She hoped she sounded reasonable as she reached for the second boot. She wasn't really going to give him a choice.

"Fine, get your boots, and come out. It's time to earn your keep, Thirteenth Warrior."

She shoved her foot into the second boot and slid out of the tent as Swindell backed up. She really wanted her sword, but she had her dagger, and hopefully, the only enemy she'd encounter that night was the crazy knight.

"So, what's the plan, Markus?" She straightened and made sure the boots fit snugly. "You think now is a good time to go into the Tombs?"

"No time like the present, *Allira*," he said cheerfully, but he jabbed at her with the sword. "Get moving."

"Okay, okay." She shoved her dagger into its scabbard and held her empty hands up in surrender. "They don't have lights or candles in there. How are we going to see the way, much less any enemies creeping up on us?"

"You'll need to fashion a torch and light it."

"With what? All my gear is in my camp."

"I'm sure you'll think of something. Now, move." He poked her between the shoulder blades with the tip of her sword.

She moved off carefully without a word, wracking her mind for anything she could do to deter the fool. He'd already caused enough damage to Mectarn and the others, and none of the knights ever came back at night. The grells and gren were resting to face the next onslaught in the morning. No one would expect humans at night.

Which may be his plan after all.

She'd walked the path to the clearing enough times to know the trail. The moonlight filtered through the canopy of trees, creating a mosaic of light on the ground in monochromatic splendor. She wished she could enjoy it, but the gate to the Tombs came into sight and he poked her back again, urging her closer.

"I got it. How are we supposed to see anything? I don't see any torch supplies lying around."

Allira hoped her voice sounded bored and annoyed instead of closing in on panic. She wished she could contact Josten for his help, but carrier pigeons didn't fly at night and she wouldn't know where to send one, anyway.

"Guess we'll have to go in the dark. I'm sure you'll be fine. Lead the way, lucky Thirteenth Warrior."

"You know there's no truth to that, right? Thirteen isn't any more lucky than ten or five, for that matter." She stumbled through the gate and hoped to hell she wouldn't be skewered.

"Oh, I know, Maplestaff. But I might as well take advantage of any luck to be had." He laughed, and the sound was ugly. "Can't have you using it all. That wouldn't be fair, now, would it?"

Allira wished she could see Swindell's face, but she had to keep her attention on the dark, yawning entrance in front of her. There was no way they'd be able to see inside the Tombs, but he didn't seem to care. She hoped she wouldn't look like a traitor to the Orcs and Goblins if—*when*—they spotted her. Nothing about this excursion was right or good, but she had to make the best of what she had.

And clobber him with a rock if I can.

But as she cleared the jumbled rocks in the entrance, the space became *brighter* than outside, despite the moonlight. She frowned and stepped around the edge of the collapsed wall to find a world of glowing blue and green.

"Whoa."

Small points of blue and green light dotted the walls and ceiling of the Caverns in glowing garlands. Some hung, waving gently in the breeze shifting through the spaces from outside, while others followed the contours of the stone arching over their heads. Swindell nudged her again, but he seemed just as amazed at the light as she was.

"This is amazing."

"Guess you got lucky after all, Maplestaff. Now we can see. Get moving."

Allira spun around until the sword was at her chest. "And where do you suppose I should go? I haven't been in here. I don't know anything about it."

Or next to nothing. Josten had led her through the warren of tunnels and chambers before. She hadn't a clue where to start looking for the Relic. Hell, she didn't even know if there really was a Relic. Josten had never mentioned it, nor had the gren or grells. All she knew about were the incredible gardens the Goblins fostered, and the village of the Orcs where they took Mectarn to find healing.

"Let's start with the throne room of the Dreadstone King, shall we?" Swindell's voice became mocking. "You know about the Dreadstone King, right, Maplestaff? The guy who had the Relic and all the treasure it hides? That's why we're here, after all. We should start there."

"All right, wise ass, which way to the throne room? I told you I've never been in here before."

"Still lying, I see. Very well, it's straight ahead—through the Maw." He pointed with his free hand, the sword never wavering, and the blue light gave him a ghastly cast. "After you."

She followed his finger to a dark hole in the wall that had stalactites hanging around it like serrated teeth waiting for its next meal. She swallowed hard. The humans had at least named it accurately. She had an unreasoning urge to turn around and dart past Swindell to freedom.

"Oh, good, I was afraid this place would be completely creepy or something." Despite her flippant words, her voice cracked as she started toward the Maw.

Swindell laughed. "You're pretty funny, Maplestaff, when you're not mouthing off to the men like you're better than them. Gods, I've wanted to shut up that smart mouth for weeks, stuff it full of my cock like it's supposed to be. Get some godsdamned peace and quiet."

She almost told him if he wanted peace and quiet, he could've started with himself and left her alone, but she'd reached the Maw and all her words dried up in her throat. No glowing lights to guide her in this part of the Tombs. It was just darkness and silence beneath the stalactites. She swallowed hard.

"What, the lucky Thirteenth Warrior is afraid of the dark?" Swindell sneered. "In you go, you treasonous bitch. Show me where the Relic is."

He reached out and shoved her into the darkness before she could reply.

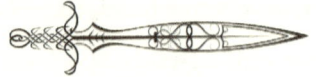

Josten cursed himself for being twelve kinds of fool. What made him think he could just reveal that he was simply the ghost of the Dreadstone King, the dusty and forgotten skeleton still seated on the stone throne with an iron crown on his cracked skull? His gut churned with the idea of Allira finding out just how ethereal he really was as he wandered the eastern fields looking for inspiration.

But I can't hide it from her if I want to be with her.

He barked an unhappy laugh. Be with her? He was dead—literally. There was no 'being with her' so long as that was true. But she had questions, and she was slowly growing suspicious. He was damn lucky he'd had the focus and energy to lift the rope latch off the gate when she asked, but it had damn near wiped him out, and made it difficult to keep his solid appearance. Which was why he'd tucked tail and run.

Despair filtered through him, and he slunk into the Tombs with a heavy heart. He passed the gren and grells getting ready for the evening meal, and asked Crent and Tral to bring hay to Allira's camp. They agreed, and he headed on with a few nods to the rest. Everyone was a little subdued—too many had been injured or killed, and Mectarn's attack was fresh on everyone's mind.

The clock was ticking on his time with Allira and his reticence about his true nature. She thought he was a friend, a companion who felt the same about the people of the Caverns. And she wasn't wrong.

Except I'm the Dreadstone King, a long dead pile of bones on a stone throne.

He should've had the courage to tell her who he was, *what* he was, and owned up to his feelings for her. In the days where they'd done domestic things like build her camp, and gather herbs, and spar, he'd fallen for her smart, practical ways. He'd watched her learn from her mistakes and take a stand against the humans who saw the Orcs and Goblins as nothing more than monsters. It all just made him want her more.

But he couldn't have her.

Josten stopped in the throne room and stared at the skeleton wearing the Iron Crown. There wasn't anything spectacular about it other than it denoted rank and rested at an odd angle on his bare skull. No one would ever know it was the very relic the humans came to the Tombs to find. The *crown* held the magic keeping him 'alive' in this twilight existence. He didn't even know how—it just did.

He stared at the throne and lost track of time, until a new sound reached his ears.

"Get in there, you treasonous bitch, and show me where the Relic is!"

Allira stumbled into view, carrying no weapons beyond her dagger, followed by a knight without a helm. His expression was an ugly scowl, and fury rolled off him like energy waves. He fairly bristled with weapons, including Allira's sword, as he strode into the throne room behind her.

She caught her balance and glanced around. Josten was so surprised to see her in the company of another human that he forgot to make himself visible. She damn near walked through him as she let her gaze slide around the throne room glowing softly in lume worm light. She looked tired but resigned as she scanned the space, but froze when her gaze landed on the throne and the skeleton.

"Oh my glory. Is *that* the Dreadstone King?" She pointed to the throne. "Has he been here the whole time?"

"I thought you've been inside the Tombs. Surely you've seen him."

"I *told* you. I've only been in the entrance. I had no idea this was here. But it sounds like you knew." She rounded on the knight. "Speaking of which, why are you *here*, Swindell? If you've searched this part of the Tombs, why did you bring me here?"

"We had to start somewhere. Besides, you're lying." The man didn't raise his voice, but fury burned in the words. "You've been in the Tombs more than just the entrance, and I *know* you've conspired with those monsters to hide the treasure, including the Relic."

She threw her hands up. "I haven't conspired with anyone! I did what I said I would—I watched your stupid horses while you made war on peaceful people. I don't know about the treasure or the Relic. And I really didn't know the Dreadstone King's skeleton was here." She peered at the throne. "Wait, is that a sword behind the chair?"

Swindell snorted as Josten shifted closer to the throne. "Why, do you think you can get to it fast enough to take me on?" He sneered. "Not only is it too big and heavy for a little girl like you, but it's been there for a century and is probably dull as shit." He waved with Allira's sword. "Start talking. I want to know where the treasure is."

"I have no idea." Allira shifted toward the throne, her eyes narrowed. "Does the sword have a double-headed horse as the pommel?"

"What does it matter? Where the fuck is the Relic?" Swindell shouted until his voice echoed in the chamber, and Josten tightened his hands into fists.

"Sshhhh!" Allira waved at the knight. "Keep your voice down. You'll wake the Orcs and Goblins, and the last thing we need is to fight them after you wounded their shaman."

Oh, the gren and grells were awake—Josten saw them creeping to the throne room, but he'd caught their attention and waved them to wait. This was the last time Swindell would make it inside the Tombs.

And he's not making it out alive.

Josten shifted toward the back of the throne while Swindell stomped closer to Allira, brandishing her sword with a snarl.

"Where is the fuckin' Relic?" He got in her face and roared the words at her. "We're not leaving until you show it to me!"

"Then you can stay here and rot, Swindell." Allira dodged the sword blade and drew her dagger. "I told you I don't have a clue where it is or even *what* it is! You're the one who's been in the Tombs, day after day, terrorizing the people here, not me. I've been *outside,* so I don't know where your fuckin' Relic or treasure is. Got it?"

Swindell's eyes narrowed, and fury tightened his features as he bared his teeth. "Then you'll die here with the rest of the loathsome creatures!"

He leapt at her, and she whirled away before striking at his arm with her dagger. Unfortunately, Swindell wore chainmail and the blade skittered off in a shower of sparks. He lost his balance a moment, but he came back with a vicious stroke that damn near took her side.

Fear and fury mixed in Josten's chest at the idea of Allira dying at the hands of a man who had no honor, no empathy, no kindness. He'd seen lifetimes' worth of death, destruction, greed, and manipulation, and he'd had enough. Josten dashed to the throne and settled himself onto the skeleton. It had been a long time since he'd animated the bones, but there was a mental snap, like a cage had been fit around him, and he opened his eyes.

Neither combatant realized he was awake as Swindell slashed at Allira again. She caught the sword with her dagger and threw it aside before twisting inside Swindell's reach and stabbing at his belly. He threw his hands wide and jerked away from her smaller blade's arc. If she'd held her sword, she would've gutted him. She spun away and took several steps out of reach as Swindell stopped with his back to the throne.

And that's my cue.

Josten steadied his energy and rose to his full height. When he'd been alive, he'd stood almost a head above most men, but as a skeletal warrior, he was much more average. However, the magic that animated him glowed with green fire licking out of his skull's eye sockets and rippling along the blade he drew from behind the throne, making him seem larger. He'd been told it was an unnerving sight, even for the gren and grells.

The sound of the blade coming free from the stone scabbard made Allira look up, and she stopped, her eyes growing round. She didn't drop her guard, but she swallowed hard and straightened as her gaze fixed on Josten. He wished he could reassure her she was in no danger from him, but his focus switched to Swindell, and his fury returned.

"You just realized you're going to die, Maplestaff?" Swindell laughed, an ugly cackle of sound ricocheting off the stalactites slowly growing into pillars. "About time."

Allira shook her head and pointed past Swindell. The man laughed again.

"That trick won't work on me. I know these Tombs well enough to know there's nothing there but an old stone throne and the skeleton." Swindell shook out his shoulders. "Let's do this."

"Yes, let's." Josten's unused voice rumbled out as he took a step closer and swung the flat of his blade into Swindell, batting him aside. "You're ready and prepared for all opponents, right?"

Swindell shook himself from where he landed and looked up, his eyes going wide. "What the fuck?"

"Not what you expected, Swindell?" Josten spread his hands as he advanced on the knight. "Really? Coming here in the dead of night, armed to the teeth with a companion who's unarmed. Did you think she'd be bait? Or were you just going to sacrifice her to your fucked up obsession for riches and power?"

Swindell scrambled to his feet as Allira shifted away, her dagger held in a white-knuckled grip. Josten wanted to tell her it would be fine, but he needed to keep his focus on the desecrator of the Tombs.

"This is bullshit. A trick of the light. You're not real."

Josten laughed, lunging two steps and swinging his sword until it clanged against Allira's, knocking it from Swindell's grip to skitter away into the shadows. "Aren't I? Doesn't that feel real to you?"

"Holy fuck!" Swindell scrambled away from Josten's second strike, but got tangled in his own scabbard and tumbled to the floor. To his credit, he rolled and managed to get to one knee, drawing his own sword. "This shit isn't real. It can't be. You're dead!"

Josten nodded. "Just figured it out, did you? Nothing gets past you." He advanced on Swindell. "Ready to join me?"

Swindell snarled and brought his blade up. "Good luck, old…" He stumbled over his words as he gestured at Josten. "Old whatever you are."

It would've been funny if Josten was in the mood to be charitable, but he'd lost his humor when Swindell brought a non-combatant into his throne room.

"Don't you recognize me, Swindell?" Josten stepped into the knight's space and struck out at him. "I'm the Dreadstone King, Demon of the Deeps, Killer of Heroes, and Keeper of the Secrets, whose throne you seek. But it will only mean your death."

He rained blows down on the human knight, and the man defended himself well enough to not die in their first bout. But Josten didn't tire. He grew stronger and more energized as he drove Swindell ahead of him around the throne room.

"Ready to give up? Ready to accept your fate?"

Swindell scowled. "Not today." He rallied and came at Josten with a flurry of blows.

Josten had to hand it to the guy—his anger overrode the fear inspired by fighting a walking skeleton draped in faded rags with green fire wafting from its eye sockets and licking up a very real blade. And the knight had skill. Granted, Josten mostly toyed with him to see just how skilled. The gren and grells of the Tombs were no slouches when it came to fighting, but Swindell and his cohorts had killed many this year.

Despite Swindell's rally and his obvious skill at fighting in close quarters, Josten wasn't worried. He was already dead, and the magic animating his skeleton would knit it back together if Swindell managed to hack off a limb. But Josten hadn't spent all those years with the Wraiths without acquiring his own set of skills.

He defended against Swindell's attack, letting the man tire himself out in his relentless blows. When he backed off to catch his breath, Josten laughed.

"Is that the best you got, Swindell? All this time wreaking havoc and destruction in the Tombs, and that's it?" Josten snorted as he stalked closer to the tired man. "You'd never have made it in the Wraiths with this lack of stamina."

"Fuck, you're old. The Wraiths haven't been around for over half a century." Swindell sneered as he returned to his fighting stance.

"I *am* old. I'm the Dreadstone King, and you've trespassed on my domain." Josten swung his flaming sword at Swindell. "You've threatened my people, and caused damage to their homes. This cannot stand."

"*Your* people? There's nothing in the Tombs other than Goblins and Orcs, monsters and nothing more." Swindell defended himself, but his sword work grew sloppy and half-hearted as his rage gave way to fear.

"They're all my people. To see them as the monsters when *you've* harmed *them* by destroying their homes shows you have no honor, no integrity, no nobility." Josten drove Swindell backwards relentlessly, giving no more quarter than the knights had given Mectarn.

"You're the very monster the tales warn about. *Humans* are the monsters."

Josten focused all his anger, his sorrow, and devastation into his sword work, hammering at the other knight. The man fought well, but he was already tired, and was no match for Josten's righteous fury. Josten batted the man's sword aside, and grasped his throat with one bony hand, yanking him close.

"Begone from this place, vile creature, and never return, and I shall let you live out your miserable life."

The man struggled in Josten's grip until he released his sword to grab Josten's bony wrist. Josten kicked the blade away and tossed the man toward the entrance to the throne room.

"You may go."

Swindell staggered and rubbed his throat with his hand as he glared. Josten picked up the dropped sword and glanced around for Allira, but she'd long disappeared. He mentally swore. It was going to take more than sharing a story around the fire to explain how he was a skeleton in rags with glowing green eyes. Of course, she might not even want to hear him out.

"No one keeps me from my rightful claim. Not the other knights, not those nasty monsters hiding my treasure, not even you."

The sound of a sword knocking against stone made Josten turn around. Swindell stood with Allira's blade in his hand and an ugly sneer pulling at his lips. He raised his chin in disdain, trying to look down his nose at Josten's greater height.

"I'll take what's mine, and I'll kill anyone who gets in my way. Starting with you."

The man launched himself at Josten, his blade swinging. But Josten ducked and swung Swindell's purloined blade, slicing the man in half through the gut. With a jerk, he severed Swindell's spine, and the body dropped with wet thuds to the floor. Swindell gaped at him, a mixture of pain, disbelief, and fear flooding his expression as he dropped Allira's sword. His mouth opened like a gasping fish, but no sound came out.

"Your time here is done, Swindell. Your rampage is ended. Begone."

Josten turned away and stomped to the throne, sheathing his sword and settling his old bones back on the stone chair.

"What was it? The...Relic...?"

Josten dipped his skull forward. "You'll never know. Welcome to the Dreadstone Tombs."

Swindell rattled his last breath, and Josten released his bones, taking up his ghostly form again. He nodded to the grells and gren waiting to deal with the offal of Swindell and swung away to find Allira. She'd long fled the throne room, but he could scent her honey and peach fragrance heading deeper into the caverns.

Chapter Fourteen

A llira fled, not even stopping to grab her discarded sword. She tried to locate the exit—the way Swindell had brought her into the throne room, but she couldn't find the passage in the darkness with the terrifying sounds of the skeletal Dreadstone King fighting with Swindell. So, she just ran any way she could.

Passages led her deeper into lume worm-lit spaces. Sometimes she thought she saw Orcs and Goblins watching from the shadows, but her panic wouldn't allow her mind to translate anything other than 'escape' and 'run.'

Eventually, her breath came in gasps and she had to stop running. She had no idea where she was or whether she was close to the exit as her feet skidded in the soft sand of the floor. It took her a few moments to realize the air was warmer, with a mineral tang common in hot springs. She braced her hands on her thighs as she tried to catch her breath and looked around.

She'd arrived in a space of warm water pools at varying heights and size, creating a wide set of overflowing shelves of curved rock cauldrons. Steps had been carved into the edges to allow for people to reach them. They looked serene and inviting, perfect for soothing away all her worries.

Yeah, well, a fuckin skeleton with blazing green eyes just started fighting Swindell—nothin's gonna soothe that!

But Allira did sink down in a corner to stare at the rippling water of the pools, softly glowing in the lume worms' light as she caught her breath. Her heart rate slowly returned to normal when the scary skeleton didn't follow her into the room, and she scrubbed her hands over her face as the details filtered back into her awareness.

Like the double horse-head pommel on the Dreadstone King's sword—just like Josten's sword. Or the pale green eyes that stared at her with recognition so similar to Josten's. Or the damn phrase the Dreadstone King used to describe himself—*the Dreadstone King, Demon of the Deeps, Killer of Heroes, and Keeper of the Secrets*. Exactly as Josten had said it.

Allira groaned.

Is Josten really the Dreadstone King?

It couldn't be true—she'd *seen* him, fought against him, gathered herbs with him. There was no way he could be a dusty skeleton with flaming eyes. Could he?

"Allira-dri?"

She gasped and looked up to find Mectarn leaning heavily on a crutch and cradling her broken arm against her side.

"Oh my glory, Mada Mectarn, what are you doing here? You should be resting." She scrambled to her feet to help the older grell find a comfortable place to sit.

"I could say the same for you. What brings you so deep into the Dreadstone Caverns?" The shaman groaned as she settled but then turned her weary eyes on Allira.

"I...I didn't come by choice. The last knight forced me through the gate to show him where the treasure was, but I don't know anything about the Caverns." She swallowed hard. "And then the skeleton with the flaming eyes showed up, and I took off."

Mectarn tilted her head. "Skeleton with the flaming eyes?"

"It sounds crazy, I know, but I swear I'm not joking. The Dreadstone King's skeleton *stood up and started fighting* with the last knight." Allira scrubbed her face again. "I think I'm losing my mind."

"The King stood up and fought? Hmm." Mectarn nodded and tapped her chin with her good hand. "He must have seen something worth the effort to defend."

Allira widened her eyes. "You believe me? I really saw the Dreadstone King fight against the invader?"

Mectarn gave her a small smirk. "You did, indeed. He very rarely makes an appearance in that form. But when he is roused, it's because someone or something needs defending."

"But Mada Mectarn, skeletons don't just get up and fight. The dead don't move... right?"

"Depends on the dead and what their mission is." Mectarm winced as she moved wrong. "Charning knights and their delusions!" She grimaced and rolled her eyes. "The Dreadstone King wasn't any different when he was a young man. He was all about power and riches and control. And it brought him nothing but cursed to live alone and lonely. If you can call his existence living."

Allira thought of all the times Mectarn and others called Josten 'Highness,' and their willingness to do things because he asked. She thought of his sword with the double horse head pommel and his weird unwillingness to talk about the Dreadstone King, and how he seemed faded or translucent a few times when she looked at him.

"Mectarn...is Josten the ghost of the Dreadstone King?"

Allira didn't quite hold her breath, but her gut churned with both hope and fear.

The Medicine Woman nodded. "He is. Did he not tell you?"

"No." Allira scowled. "He pretty much avoided the subject each time I brought it up."

Mectarn sighed. "For such a fierce warrior and a powerful king, he lets his fear control him too many times when it comes to things that are important." She gestured at one of the pools close to them. "Perhaps you'd help me into the pool? The water has healing properties for my people, and I could use the respite from pain."

"Of course." Allira scrambled to her feet and held her hands out to the injured woman.

Mectarn took her hand and levered herself up until she could hobble to the pool. Allira unwrapped the grell's excess robes before offering help climbing into the pool. When Mectarn settled with a sigh, Allira took her boots off and stuck her feet in the bubbling mineral water.

"Oh, that's lovely." She shot Mectarn a rueful smile. "I had no idea these were here. If you ask me, they're the true treasure of the Tombs. Imagine coming in after a hard day of fighting or working. I could sit here for hours."

"You're not wrong. Many of the gren and grells use them for just that." Mectarn closed her eyes and rested her head against the lip of the pool for a few moments, and the silence between them deepened.

But Allira's mind kept turning over the problem of Josten being a ghost or a re-animated skeleton. Either way, her connection to him was based on a fundamental misunderstanding—one he'd chosen not to correct. Where did that leave them? Where did it leave *her*?

She'd fallen for him, for the man who liked reading the tales of Torsha the Bold by firelight. The man who helped her make her camp more comfortable and decorative. The man who sparred with her—

"How could Josten spar with me when he's just a ghost?"

"He's not 'just a ghost,' Allira-dri. If that was all he was, he wouldn't have been able to move his bones or bring you that book." At Allira's raised eyebrows, Mectarn nodded. "Oh yes, I've been aware of his courtship of you for a while now."

Allira snorted. "Courtship."

"It's his way of showing you he cares. Sure, it's clumsy and lacking clear communication, but it was his attempt to show you his interest and his affection."

"But he's a ghost." She laughed a little and scrubbed her face again. "I can't believe I'm saying this unironically. He's a ghost, of a long dead king. This is insane."

"Yes, he's a ghost and you love him. What of it?"

"I've heard of women marrying ghosts, but I chalked it up to the ladies being desperate either to be with someone or get away from someone else." Allira blinked as her mind caught up with Mectarn's words. "Wait, what? I never said anything about love."

Mectarn shot her a perplexed smile. "You didn't? Hmm, I could've sworn I heard it in the words you said and the distress you're feeling. But I'm just an old shaman grell, soaking her aching bones in the mineral baths."

Allira snorted again. "Yeah, okay, whatever. I'm not buying that bushel of horseshit."

Mectarn laughed, then winced. "Oh, you mustn't make me laugh. My ribs are still broken."

"Sorry." Allira took a deep breath and hunched her shoulders as she leaned on her hands gripping the lip of the pool. "I thought I loved him—love him—but now it seems impossible. I mean, I'm an out-of-work mercenary who doesn't want to fight anymore, and he's the ghost of the Dreadstone King who can turn into a flame-eyed, walking skeleton. There's a lot to unpack there."

Mectarn grunted thoughtfully. "Actually, you both sound perfect for each other."

Allira barked a laugh in spite of herself. "Lady Won't-Fight and Lord Can't-Fight? Yeah, we're a match made in heaven."

"I shall have to remember those nicknames." Mectarn grinned as Allira shook her head. "But both of you *can* fight should the time call for it." She reached over and patted Allira's ankle. "What really bothers you, Lady Dreadstone?"

"Uh, he's a ghost?"

Mectarn raised an eyebrow, which looked lopsided with the swelling on her face.

Allira sighed. "I guess... I guess I'm just unnerved with the fact that the man I love isn't physically present. I can't touch him. On the other hand, I fell in love with him without physical intimacy, so I really have nothing to complain about."

"Mm." Mectarn swirled her good hand in the water. "What if you *could* have physical intimacy?"

"Dreams don't count," Allira said tartly.

"Dreams? Did you have a dream about Josten?"

"Uhm..." Allira glanced away toward the lume worms hanging from the ceiling. "I find my memory's not what it was. I'll have to get back to you on that."

Mectarn chuckled. "Fair enough. Keep your secrets, but I wasn't referring to dreams. Are you familiar with the Dreadstone King legend?"

Allira shrugged. "Sort of. I mean, he was said to be a ruthless ruler, power-hungry and cunning. The legend states he amassed a large fortune of gold and jewels, and stored them here in the Tombs before he died. It goes on to say that he had a Relic that grants anyone who finds it access to the land, the treasure, and everlasting life, or some such crap. I didn't really pay attention beyond the stories told to the knights so they'd sign on for the annual suicide mission."

"Perhaps it's a good thing your people don't know the real story." Mectarn glanced over her shoulder as if looking for listeners and Allira shivered. "The Dreadstone King was ruthless and power-hungry. So much so, he abandoned the only found family he had in order to stay as the King of the Dreadstone Caverns. He did amass treasure, but it wasn't necessarily gold and jewels, and for a time, his kingdom was prosperous. However, one can only be that way for so long before it starts to crumble and people get tired of feeding one man's ego and fear."

"He sounds awful, but Josten doesn't seem to be that man anymore." Allira snorted. "Of course, he's a ghost, so I guess he's not a man at all."

"Oh, he's a man, all right, with all the foibles of men." Mectarn rolled her eyes and grimaced. "When his people grew tired of his tirades and antics, they started to leave. What once was a prosperous city and kingdom gradually emptied out. But the Dreadstone King stayed, hoarding his power and riches until only he remained, alone, paranoid, starving, and still just as power-hungry as before, sure everyone was out to get him."

Allira widened her eyes. "Did he just sit on that damn throne and waste away?"

"Not quite. He'd acquired the Iron Crown, he thought it would bring him notoriety and prestige. What he didn't realize was it was an artifact of power, but only for the bearer. It grants the wearer longevity for as long as they need to atone for grievous wrongs committed in life. Once they have atoned, made reparations, the curse releases them."

Allira blinked. "You just described the story The Curse of the Rusty Crown told by Torsha the Bold."

"Oh? Torsha must have come across the Iron Crown before Josten, but was wise enough not to put it on." Mectarn stared meditatively at her hands in the water. Her polished stone bracelets flashed in the soft glowing light of the lume worms.

"So, Josten put it on, and lost his kingdom and his body, but was stuck here as a ghost?" Allira shivered. "That would be awful."

"A rather fitting atonement for what he'd done in his life. But when the Goblins, Orcs, Nagas, and mineral salamanders found a home in the Dreadstone Caverns, he had a new kingdom to rule over—and no desire to rule." Mectarn smirked. "Apparently, he'd realized he wasn't much of a leader."

"But you all call him Highness when you talk to him."

Mectarn shrugged. "It had been his rank, and his skeleton still sat on the throne with the Iron Crown on its head. Seemed fitting."

"It's rather ironic, I would think." Allira kicked her feet in the warm water. "So, if Josten has to atone for all the horrible things he did as the Dreadstone King, do you think he's done enough? Or is there some special thing he must do to be free of the curse?"

"That is the question, isn't it? What do you think, Highness? Is there something more you need to do to allow the Iron Crown to release you?"

Allira looked up and met Josten's turbulent gaze.

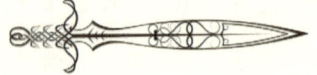

Allira scrambled out of the water and stood back as Josten stepped into the light of the lume worms. He'd retreated to his usual self, with the shoulder length dark hair, matching dark beard, red riveted doublet and fur-shouldered cloak.

"Highness."

He hated hearing the distant politeness in her voice, but he nodded. "Allira."

"Come join us, Highness." Mectarn patted the stone beside her pool. "There's space for one more if you'd like to relax."

Allira didn't look relaxed, but she did appear to be calmer than she was when he'd first stood up with his flaming sword. He found a relatively dry shelf the settle on close to Mectarn's pool and sat, hoping Allira would return to her seat.

"Has the last knight been dealt with?" Mectarn winced as she repositioned in the pool, but she already looked better than earlier that day.

"He has. He won't be bothering anyone again."

"Did you kill him?"

Josten raised his gaze to meet Allira's. "I did."

"Good." She nodded sharply. "He wasn't going to stop and he couldn't be reasoned with."

"I noticed that. I did give him the opportunity to leave with his life, but he wouldn't be deterred." Josten shrugged. "He would've made a good candidate for the Iron Crown's Curse, but he probably would've made it miserable for everyone else."

"That's certainly true." Mectarn nodded. "If you hadn't killed him, the Orcs would have."

"They've suffered enough. It was my turn to take care of them."

Mectarn gave him a wise smile full of approval. "You've done a lot of that over the years. You've even taken care of Allira-dri while she stayed near the Caverns. You've made an excellent ruler to the people here; better, I suspect, than you were to the humans."

He gave a short, humorless laugh. "No question about it."

"Why didn't you tell me?"

Allira's quiet question dropped into the soft trickling of the water in the pools, and Josten raised his gaze to meet hers. "Tell you what?"

"That you were a ghost! That you were the Dreadstone King! What the hell, Josten?"

Her voice grew louder as she reached the last question and she threw her hands out.

"I wanted to—"

"You *wanted* to, but just didn't bother to do it? That was kinda vital information, don't you think?"

"How was I going to tell you, Allira?" He rose to his feet. "Hey, good to see you. Thanks for hanging out with me. Oh, by the way, I'm the Dreadstone King and a ghost, but you know, it's all good now. It's not exactly something I can just casually bring up in conversation."

"What about when you said, and I quote, Dreadstone King, Demon of the Deeps, Killer of Heroes, and Keeper of the Secrets? You didn't think it would've been a good time to mention you had a connection to him? To *you*? What *other* secrets do I need to be aware of?"

"Okay, I made that last one up, but it isn't far from the truth. But that's the only real secret I got."

"We've spent days together. You didn't think it was something I needed to know? And we *sparred*! How the hell did that happen if you're a ghost?"

"I can concentrate and make parts of me solid when necessary." *Especially if I'm thinking illicit thoughts about someone.* But he didn't say that part aloud.

"Oh my glory, none of this makes sense." Allira spun away from him, her hands in fists at her sides, but she turned back and pointed at him. "Ghosts don't exist!"

He spread his hands. "All evidence to the contrary."

"And what about the skeleton? Do you just slip into something more boney for special occasions?"

"Well…yeah."

"It's not funny, Josten. You scared the shit outta me. And I didn't even want to be there!"

"That's kind of the point, isn't it? The Tombs are supposed to be scary. That's why they're full of dead things."

"All right, you're both wearing me out." Mectarn shifted her weight and grimaced. "I'm too tired and in pain to listen to you work this dreck out, so I'm going to skip to the part where you both say what you really want. Yes? Good. Josten, you go first."

He blinked. "First for what?"

Mectarn growled. "Don't play dumb, Highness. I don't have the time. Tell her what you want."

It was rare for Mectarn to reprimand anyone, and though he deserved it, he wasn't ready to admit everything to Allira for fear of her rejection. But the look Mectarn gave him said she knew exactly what he was thinking and she didn't care.

Josten cleared his throat and met Allira's gaze. "I want more time."

"What?" She frowned.

"I want more time. With you. I want a life with you. I want sunrises and tea in the morning, and I want to sit by the fire and read books with you as the sun goes down." He gave her a look of entreaty. "I want time with you to be a true partnership and protect the Tombs from invaders. I'd even help with the War Horsey Rides."

"But you're dead."

"Not entirely." Mectarn pulled herself out of the pool and sat on its edge as she gave Allira a half-smile. "The curse only keeps him in this state until he fulfills its purpose, then he's free to make a choice of life or true death." She pulled on her discarded robes.

Allira shook her head then scrubbed her face. "Not entirely? Are you going to tell me he's 'mostly dead'? Because I've seen the skeleton." She paused and smirked a moment, her gaze sliding over to Josten. "Good bones."

Josten couldn't help the laugh that erupted.

"We'll get to that." Mectarn waved her concerns away with a sharp gesture. "But first, we need to hear what you truly want, Allira."

"What *I* want? What does that have to do with anything?"

"It has to do with everything—the past, the future, but most importantly, the present."

Allira narrowed her eyes. "I don't understand. I didn't want to be here. I *never* wanted to be here."

"And yet you came."

"I didn't have a choice!"

Mectarn snorted. "You always have a choice, Allira-dri. You made the choice to come to the Dreadstone Caverns, but stay outside. You made the choice to befriend the denizens of the Caverns instead of supporting the knights. All of these are the choices *you* made. Now, you must make another."

Allira dropped her chin and crossed her arms over her chest. "Which is?"

"You must choose to do the same thing over and over, going back to your old life; or choose something completely different, and possibly better, despite the unknowns. The choice is yours."

Mectarn struggled to rise, and Josten concentrated on making himself solid enough to help her. "Thank you, Highness. I'm better, but the damage is extensive."

"I should've killed the bastards when they first arrived." He growled as he helped her over to a dry perch and wrapped a drying cloth around her lower body.

"No, then lessons wouldn't have been learned, nor friends gained." She tightened the towel with her good hand.

"Friends wouldn't have been *lost*, either."

She nodded. "No, but this will be the last year of loss from such events." She glanced up at Josten. "This could be the end of many things if you have the courage, Highness."

"I don't want to go back to my old life." Allira stated it carefully as if testing the truth of her words.

"What *do* you want?" Mectarn fixed her golden gaze on Allira with frank interest.

"I want..." Allira's gaze strayed to Josten. "I want to stay here with my garden and my herd of horses. I want to make a life doing something other than fighting and killing. And I want..." She bit her lip and tightened her arms against her body. "I want a friend and partner who doesn't run away every time something gets hard to talk about."

Josten resisted the urge to dig his toe into the mud around the pools.

"I think that's fair." Mectarn nodded. "What do you say, Highness?"

Josten blinked. "What do I say? I think those are admirable things."

Mectarn closed her eyes and heaved a breath before rubbing her eyes with her good hand. "Highness, you're the most vexing male I've dealt with in a long time."

Allira laughed, and Josten shook his head. "What?"

"Let me spell it out for you." Mectarn's voice grew patient, like one explaining a concept to a child. "You donned the Iron Crown, so you made choices when you were younger you wouldn't make today. But you've spent your undead life helping the denizens of the Caverns protect their homes. You even befriended an invading knight and helped her set up a temporary home and find her new purpose. You've done your time, Highness. You've worn the Iron Crown, but I heard the system break when you put others before yourself. Now you must choose which ending you want."

"Ending?" He couldn't help his jaw dropping.

"Oh my glory! The Curse of the Rusty Crown." Allira turned wide eyes to him. "'The Crown's gifts are dearly bought, it requires atonement in trade, for all the actions the wearer has wrought, only in kindness are the debts repaid.' Torsha the Bold found the Iron Crown before and wrote about it. But Josten, the curse is broken because of your *kindness*, because of all the things you've done to help. Mectarn's saying you get to choose to die for real or live a new life."

The words didn't make sense. They were perfectly clear, but his mind couldn't wrap around their meaning. They heralded a change in understanding and existence, a cataclysmic shift in his way of being, and he couldn't process the possibility.

"Josten?" Allira waved at him. "Are you hearing me? You get to choose what happens next."

"I...I don't know how."

Her brow wrinkled. "What do you mean you don't know how? You just choose what you want. You said you wanted more time, right? More time with me. Right?"

Josten froze, caught in the lightning bolt of understanding. He couldn't process anything more than surprise, and he lost his grip on his solidity. The bathing cave faded from view and he found himself in the darkness of the throne room, staring at the skeleton still propped on the throne.

I'm free...? Finally free to make a choice?

The questions ran over and over again in his head, and he collapsed at the foot of the throne, his mind not quite believing the development. He didn't feel any different, and his body remained somewhat transparent, a ripple in someone's vision instead of a solid form. How could the curse be broken if he still looked like this?

"You're a gronk!"

Mectarn's voice cracked like a whip, and Josten lurched to his feet as she threw a rock at the throne.

"What the hell was that for?"

"For your stupidity! For the dreck you pulled. For all of it!" She hobbled into the throne room with Gundri holding a torch over her to light the way. "What the charn's wrong with you?"

He grunted. "Other than being a ghost attached to a dusty skeleton? Not much."

"Don't be snide with me, Highness. I don't have the time or patience for it." She pointed her good hand at him. "You just lost your chance to tell Allira-dri how you truly feel, and you faded out to this gods-forsaken place. I can't believe she was right. She said you ran away from anything hard, and so you did. Are you completely daft?"

"What?" He looked around. "How long have I been gone?"

"Long enough for me to find Gundri, light a torch, and hobble here all the way from the bathing rooms." She scowled and shook her head. "If I didn't know you hadn't meant to charn up, I would've left you here with your gods-forsaken curse to live with the consequences of your stupidity."

Josten took a step back, surprise at Mectarn's vehemence widening his eyes. She'd never spoken to him with such anger before, and she wasn't backing down.

"That woman loves you, you absolute gronk! She was even willing to see beyond your ethereal form, accepting you're a ghost, and show hope that you might get your choice, even if it means you choose death. And what did you do?" She pointed a clawed finger at him as her lips drew back from her long canines. "You *ran away*. You acted like a gods-damned coward. Have you learned *nothing*?"

"I didn't run away. I'm right here like I always am." He threw his hands out. "And I'm not a coward."

"Oh really? Where did you run to, *Highness*?" She said it with dripping disdain. "Back to your throne, your Iron Crown? Good for you. It's your security blanket, then. Do you know what Alli-ra-dri saw? Take a wild guess, I dare you."

He opened his mouth, but she cut him off.

"She saw you fade away into nothing. What's she to think, Josten? After asking you to confirm that you wanted more time *with her*, you up and disappeared. Can you guess how that made her feel? Can you surmise what she did next?"

His mouth suddenly dried out, and he swallowed hard. "What did she do?"

"She went home after asking one of the grells to escort her out of the Caverns so she didn't disturb them. Where were you, Josten?"

He cleared his throat. "I was here."

"You were here." Mectarn nodded. "You were here with your tail between your legs, forsaking the one person who helped you reach the position of *having* a choice. Sweet glory, Josten, you have a choice now, and you ran from it. And *her*."

"I'm sorry!" His voice thundered in the space, but instead of sounding imposing or mighty, it sounded petulant and frustrated. "It's a lot to take in. I wasn't prepared for the choice—I didn't think it would ever happen and I couldn't process it. I lost focus and ended up here. I wasn't running away, I just wasn't thinking."

"Well, *start* thinking. Make a gods-damned decision, because you're out of time."

Josten narrowed his eyes. "What's that supposed to mean?"

"It means the curse is broken, but eventually the gods will take the decision away from you." Mectarn waved at the skeleton on the throne. "Your body has been dead a long time, Josten. Over seven decades by my reckoning. The curse kept your skeleton intact for all that time. But now, the curse is broken, the magic is waning, and you've made no choices about your future. You must choose or lose everything. And I do mean, everything this time. Allira-dri will leave."

Panic rose in his chest, and he swung toward the front of the throne room. He had to get to Allira before she packed her things and left the Dreadstone Hills. He had to speak to her and apologize, and tell her everything in his heart before she disappeared forever.

"She won't see you, Josten." Mectarn's voice sounded sad.

He turned to look at the shaman. "What are you talking about?"

"Your time's up. You have to make a choice. Start a new life as a man or pass beyond the veil. You can't leave the Caverns until it's been made." Mectarn hobbled closer and stood beside him, her gaze clashing with his. "It's time, Josten."

He looked back at the skeleton in its rags, sagging on the throne with the Iron Crown on its head. "What about the crown? What will happen to it?"

Mectarn shrugged. "That all depends on you. If you choose to depart this world, we will toss it in the deepest hole we can find and hope it doesn't find a new wearer. If you choose to live again with Allira-dri, you may find a place to put it that keeps it safe. But it's time to make the choice."

She rested a hand on his shoulder and for the first time ever, he felt the weight and heat of it. It made him blink in surprise. How could he feel anything? He was a ghost. Wasn't he?

She grunted. "Ah, I see you've made your decision after all."

He whipped around to look at her. "What?"

Mectarn nodded at her hand on his shoulder. "You're growing solid, Highness. Now, let's make it permanent, and then you can go apologize to Allira-dri."

He swallowed hard. Permanent. No longer ethereal. He took a deep breath, feeling his chest expand with it, and nodded. "Okay."

"Right, then, close your eyes. This might feel odd."

Mectarn raised her good hand and began muttering in Goblin. Her hand began to glow like a star, bright and burning, and Josten hurriedly closed his eyes, trying to shield himself from the light.

His heartbeat rushed in his ears, and his skin sweated in the heat coming off the Medicine Woman as she pointed her hand, fingers spread, at him. Her muttering grew louder, and the heat grew more intense until there was a weird snapping sensation.

Pain filtered through his system in a momentary spike, making him scream, then he fell into the light.

Chapter Fifteen

Allira shuffled out the front entrance of the Tombs into the windy night and smelled water in the air. The trees rattled in the increased breeze and thunder sounded in the distance.

Storm coming.

She snorted with disdain. That was an understatement. She had a lot she wanted to rail at Josten, but she was just too damn tired. She stumbled through the clearing, still managing to find the trail through the trees to her camp in the dark. Too bad she didn't have her sword—that bastard Swindell had taken it into the Tombs with him and there was no way in hell she'd go back for it.

Maybe there's still a decent blade left by one of the dead knights.

But she didn't really believe her own words. Besides, she was done being a warrior-for-hire. What did she need a sword for anymore? She grimaced as she forced her tired body to follow the trail back to her camp. The only reason she knew she'd reached it was the smell of horse manure and the looming Dreadstone Hills black against the lighter gray sky.

She wanted to drop straight into sleep and forget about the ugly events of the evening—particularly the end of it—but her mind wouldn't shut down. She lit a fire in the fire pit and started tea in the kettle before the rain started. Grabbing a blanket from her bed, she settled down in front of the fire and wrapped it around her shoulders.

The hissing of the rain in the fire sounded like the hope draining from her life, protesting all the way. Because when she told Josten he had the chance for more time with her, he literally faded from sight and disappeared.

If that isn't an ego crusher, I don't know what is.

Lightning flashed across the sky over the trees and the wind kicked up, matching her flash of frustration and irritation. The boom of thunder came several seconds later, but the kettle boiled and she was able to make her tea before the rain sheeted down. She retreated to her lean-to and sat in her tent with her tea, staring glumly out at the roiling storm extinguishing her fire.

Usually, storms and tea made her feel all warm and cozy, but disappointment sank into her bones and pulled down the corners of her mouth. She wasn't sure where the disappointment came from most. The end of her time at the Tombs? Returning to Capstone Creek as a farmer with her grandmothers? Josten's literal fade-out when she restated his interest in more time with her? All of the above?

The rain pounded her camp with a wall of dark silver spreading across the open space where the horses huddled under the trees closest to the camp. She suddenly wished she'd asked the gren and grells to have extended her overhang to cover the firepit, but hoped she'd be able to re-light it after the storm. She set her tea down beside her bed and curled into a ball, pulling her blankets over her as she watched the rain.

Sure enough, the deluge doused the fire and swamped her camp, but the lean-to kept the worst of it off her tent. Allira fell asleep to the pattering of the rain.

She woke with the sounds of water dropping off the edge of the lean-to and the fresh breeze rattling the trees. She sat up and scrubbed the sleep from her eyes, taking the time to fully come back into her body. She'd slept hard, like she hadn't rested in days, and given the whole reason she'd come to Dreadstone, it seemed accurate.

Someone whickered from the corral, and she forced herself to get up. She ignored the grimy feeling and wondered if Mectarn would let her back in the Caverns to use the bathing pools. The Goblin woman had given her a sympathetic look when Josten had disappeared and left Allira standing with her jaw hanging open. It had been surreal—she'd tried to clarify his interest in her and he'd just gone *poof!*

What do you mean you don't know how? You just choose what you want. You said you wanted more time, right? More time with me. Right?

Her words mocked her as they echoed in her head. She sat up and stuffed her feet in her boots, grimacing at the cold damp. Then she threw her cloak over her shoulders and went out into the drippy morning, trying to ignore the deep ache in her chest.

It was fine. She would be fine. She'd lived without Josten her whole life, and he'd been a ghost the whole time she was at the Tombs, which meant he wasn't really there, anyway. One couldn't become attached to a ghost.

Yeah, keep telling yourself that.

Allira straightened her shoulders and went to check on the horses. She threw out hay for them and rubbed Javalina's nose when the gelding came to the edge of the fence. She tried to ignore the heaviness in her heart as she looked around the space that had become her place. Strangely, despite its rather rudimentary construction, it had become her home, moreso than the farm in Capstone Creek.

She bit her lip. Maybe the Goblins would allow her to stay whether she was involved with Josten or not.

Given that he literally disappeared instead of answer my question, it's definitely not.

But she liked Mectarn and Gundri, Crent, Tral, even grumpy Ulfer who'd originally ordered her to never enter the Tombs. They were good people however inhuman, and she could learn a lot from them. She'd rather hang out with them than most humans any day.

She patted Javalina's neck in farewell and went back to rekindle her fire. It would be a long, cold, wet day if she couldn't get the fire started for tea or a warm meal. She glanced at her lean-to. Maybe she could ask the Orcs to help her build a little cabin—something with windows and a door so she could keep out the wind but let in the light.

After much digging and effort, she finally got the mud out of her firepit and laid mostly-dry kindling in the base to light her fire. She wanted tea and flat cakes, but settled for the warmth of the fire and some dried meat while she waited for the flames to get going. She closed her eyes and listened to the water drip off the branches of the trees as she tightened her cloak around her.

Beyond the dripping branches and the wind, it was quiet, and she tried to let it absorb her sorrow.

Until a horse whickered in greeting and she heard footsteps coming up the path. She opened her eyes and glanced over her shoulder, prepared to offer greetings to one of her neighbors.

The man walking toward her camp was tall, dark-haired, with a trimmed beard, and broad shoulders. He wore a burgundy doublet with matching bracers and a fur-edged cloak over his shoulders. Well-tooled boots flashed with each step beneath canvas trousers that encased his thighs.

At first, Allira thought it was Josten's ghost coming to give her a final farewell, but then she noticed the beads of water on the fur of his cloak and the wind ruffling his hair. He grimaced and shoved it behind his ears in irritation, and she couldn't help the inward smile at the very human reactions.

"Good morning, Allira."

She nodded to him before turning back to her sputtering fire. "Good morning."

"How'd you sleep?" He stopped on the other side of her fire, but she kept her gaze on the weak flames.

"Fine. Deep. I was really tired."

"Yes, I imagine."

The inane conversation made her tired, and she leaned her elbows on her knees. "What do you want, Josten?"

He must have heard the lack of welcome in her voice. "I, uh, I came to bring you this. And to apologize."

She finally looked up and found him holding out her sword, the one Swindell had stolen from her. She frowned. He held it out to her and it didn't waver. Neither did he, which she chalked up to his remarkable control as a ghost. She rose and took the sword from him.

"Thanks." She set it aside against the wall of the lean-to. "You came to apologize?"

He nodded and tucked his hair behind his ears again. "Yes. Mectarn informed me I simply faded out last night, and left you hanging with no answers to your questions. That was terribly rude, and I'm very sorry."

"How very formal of you. I appreciate you taking the time to apologize."

He grimaced. "Sorry, I get really formal when I'm nervous. It was one of the things the guys in the Wraiths would tease me about."

She gave him a half-hearted laugh. "Right, the Wraiths, when you were alive a hundred years ago."

"Yeah..." He rubbed the back of his neck. "May I sit down? I'd forgotten how heavy a body can be."

She frowned but nodded, gesturing to one of the other stumps as her kettle boiled. She rose to take it off the fire and watched Josten flare out his cloak so he didn't end up sitting on it. The stump rocked a little as he settled, and she wondered why he was putting so much effort into his performance.

She dismissed his actions and poured hot water into her mug before setting the kettle on the cooling stone and retaking her seat.

"Aren't you going to offer me some tea?"

Allira shook her head. "Ghosts don't drink tea."

"I'm not a ghost."

She glanced up over the rim of her mug, studying him. The wind ruffled his hair again, making him push it out of his eyes, and resettle his cloak over his lap. Could it be true? Was he truly sitting across the fire from her?

She set her mug down on the ground and rose, her gaze taking in all the details of his costume and position. Including the dirt on his boots that appeared to be fresh from walking from the Caverns in the mud.

But he was good at making himself seem solid.

"Prove it."

Josten rose and straightened his clothes before stepping around the fire straight into her space. Allira didn't budge. She met his gaze without a smile. With all the untruths she'd dealt with over the last few weeks, she wasn't just taking things on faith anymore.

"First, I need your permission." He studied her expression, and she noted his hair looked real. "May I kiss you?"

That wasn't a question she expected, but she nodded.

He reached up and cupped her head with gentle hands. He smelled like fresh rainwater and summer pine in the sun, warm, spicy, and eternal. The heat of his hands seeped into her skin, and her shoulders relaxed for the first time that morning.

Then he leaned in and she closed her eyes as he brushed his lips against hers.

Heat, power, and the soft brush of his beard sent pleasure rushing through her, and she remembered her dream. But this was better. She gasped when she realized she could feel the strength and hardness of his body when she wrapped her arms around his waist.

He was solid. He was warm. And he was kissing her.

He slid a hot tongue into her mouth and caressed hers as he tilted his head to get closer. Pleasure flared and ran straight to her pussy, making her nipples tighten against her shirt.

And then it was over. He pulled back and met her gaze.

"Sweet glory," she whispered.

"I agree. I've been waiting for days to do that." Josten gave her a self-deprecating smile.

"So, I guess this means you've made your decision."

He barked a surprised laugh. "I have."

"Congratulations. May I have another?" Her voice sounded pleading, even to her.

He laughed again. "It would be my pleasure." And he kissed her again.

This time, it was more intense, as if he wanted to know everything about her, stroking and nipping at her lips. He tilted his head to deepen their connection, and every caress lit her on fire. Her nipples tingled, and her pussy clenched with aching desire.

No one had ever kissed her in such a way, and she fell into the sensations before her logical brain caught up with her. She wanted more kisses, more touches, more physical connections that had only been in her dreams and wishes before. He deepened the kiss, but made it gentle, teasing, and she didn't want it to stop.

When he finally pulled back to let her breathe, he stared down at her, searching her expression.

"Wow."

"I couldn't have said it better."

She swallowed hard. "Still want some tea?"

He met her gaze steadily. "I do. I haven't tasted it in decades."

She snorted and gave a little nervous laugh. "I guess that's probably true."

She expected him to resume his seat across the fire from her, but instead he settled on the rock beside her stump and accepted the cup of tea. She sat down with her own mug, strangely comforted by the heat coming off his body beside her. They didn't say anything for a few moments as he tasted the tea, and she watched his expression for his reaction.

"Mm, what is this?"

She shrugged. "A mint combo from my grandmothers' garden. They dried it themselves."

"It's really good. Refreshing." He swallowed it and held out the mug. "May I have more?"

Allira grinned. "You may." She took his mug and poured hot water into it before adding the tea leaves. "Let it steep for a few minutes. It makes it taste better."

"Oh, right. Yeah, I forgot it takes a little bit of time." He held the mug close and sniffed the steam. "I like being able to taste things again."

She laughed. "Just wait until you get hungry. Then it's not nearly as great." She glanced at her lean-to. "Speaking of which, I need to figure out what's going to happen next."

He lowered his tea to his lap. "What do you mean?"

She grimaced. "I'm almost out of food. I don't have a garden or supplies to last a winter out here, and there aren't any settlements nearby except for the Caverns dwellers. And you know how they feel about humans right now."

He waved her worries away. "I'll talk to them."

She barked another laugh. "Josten, you do know you're not a ghost anymore, right? I'm not convinced they won't see you as a threat now that you're corporeal again. Aren't you as human as me now?"

"I am..." He nodded, his expression thoughtful. "But despite my species, they know me as the being that I was. Like they know you. Your actions spoke to them, like mine have while I was a ghost."

"Did they all know you were a ghost?"

He blinked. "I...I don't know. I thought they all knew, but maybe only Mectarn did." He scoffed and shook his head. "No, surely they all knew."

"How will they react to you *not* being a ghost now? Will they even know the difference?"

He glanced down and ran his fingers over the mug. "I don't know. This is new for me. I'm used to the old ways of doing things and now, I'm hungry and thirsty and tired for the first time in decades."

Allira snorted. "Yeah, having a body is tiring. And eating is a pain in the ass."

He nodded. "I never realized just how heavy it is. Like the Iron Crown but worse."

"You haven't experienced the delight of pulling your back by sleeping, or sneezing. That's a joy and a half." She smirked before she finished her own tea and sighed. "So, what's going to happen now? You're human again and as I said, I'm almost out of food."

"I'm not sure I follow. What's the problem?"

"I can't feed myself on what I have here, there's no human settlement nearby to trade with—if I *had* something to trade—and you're going to need to eat, too, now that you're alive." She gazed out at the horses stirring in the misty morning. "I don't want to leave here. It's been a sanctuary despite the whole reason for coming." She sighed and looked back at him. "But I have to tell my grandmothers what happened to me, and I should probably bring the bits of personal items from the knights back to Capstone Creek. Then I can report there's no treasure or relic, and the humans can stop invading."

Josten snorted. "I doubt it'll be that easy."

She gave him a rueful smile. "They can't really argue with someone who's been here and dumps the dead knights' junk at their feet, now, can they?"

"Town magistrates aren't known for their common sense, but I appreciate your interest in trying to convince them." Josten finished his tea and set his mug aside before he grasped her hand. "But I have a suggestion before you pack up and leave."

Allira met his gaze. "And that is?"

"Let's talk to Mectarn and the Council of Elders about staying. As I said before, they were very impressed with you and agreed it might be useful to have a human nearby. I think we could convince them of the use of having us both here, not only as helpful neighbors, but also as guards against incursions from other humans. Then you can keep your sanctuary and have a home to return to after you travel to Capstone Creek."

She raised an eyebrow. "You're speaking formally again. What's making you nervous?"

He rubbed the back of his head with one hand. "We shared a kiss, Allira, but we've said nothing about it. Now we talk of a future—something I never considered, I might add—and yet, it's not certain that there will be a 'we' in that future."

She tilted her head and rubbed her chin. "Rather than pussy-footing around, let me be blunt. Do you want a future with me?"

She'd never seen Josten caught completely flatfooted as his jaw dropped and his eyes widened. But to his credit he snapped his mouth shut and nodded quickly.

"Yes."

"All right, then." She set down her tea and rose, turning to face him. She held out her hand for his mug, and set it with the other when he handed it to her. "Here's the deal, Josten. I'm not waiting a century for you to get a clue. I'm going to make the assumption that you kissing me was a sign that you want more." She dipped her head so she could meet his gaze. "And to be clear, I *do* want a future with 'we' and 'us' in it."

Relief washed over his expression. "Thank goodness."

"Damn right, it'll be goodness. Because we're staying here, together, and we're going to make damn sure there's no more Relic hunts. Right?"

He nodded, his smile relaxing.

She narrowed her eyes. "Speaking of relics, where is the Iron Crown now?"

"I honestly don't know." He smirked at her surprised look. "Mectarn took it and said she had just the place for it, but wouldn't tell me where that was. Personally, I think she dropped it in one of the brine pools of the Caverns. There it will stay, being encrusted with minerals, buried for all time. But I don't actually know."

Allira nodded. "That's an excellent place for it. And not knowing where it ended up is just fine for me. Some secrets are best en-earthed, so-to-speak."

Josten laughed. "So-to-speak."

She grinned. "So, now that the relic is taken care of, how soon do we have to go talk to the Council of Elders about staying?"

He frowned. "As soon as you'd like. Why?"

She spread her legs and straddled his lap with a saucy grin. "Because now that I have you here, in the flesh"—he snorted—"I'd like to have some time getting to know the real you."

He blinked before a smirk curled his lips. "Getting to know me, eh? You mean, physically?"

"Damn straight." She tilted her head and pressed her lips to his.

Josten groaned and wrapped his arms tightly around her as he gave into her kiss. He might have been a ghost for a century, but he could still kiss. He slid his tongue into her mouth, and a shiver ran down her back. Delicious heat flooded from her chest to her pussy as his tongue caressed hers.

She pulled back long enough to meet his gaze, his pupils dilated so wide the color appeared almost gone.

"I really like the way you kiss me."

The smirk returned to his face. "Good. I really like kissing you. But I do have a suggestion."

She raised her eyebrows. "Oh?"

"Yeah, can we get out of the rain? I'm not used to being affected by the weather and the rain is cold. And I want to see more than just your beautiful smile."

Allira glanced up and rain sprinkled across her cheeks. "Um, yeah, that's a good point." She pushed off his lap. "Come into my lean-to tent. Just remember to remove your boots."

He rose fluidly and followed after her, his expression intense. "I shall remove anything you wish."

She grinned. "Good. I was hoping that would be the case. Start with the boots."

She showed him by sitting down just inside the overhang and pulling her boots off before setting them to the side out of the rain. Then she crawled into the tent proper and sat on her bedroll. He followed her lead, but when he crawled inside, he paused to close the tent flap to keep the wind and rain out.

Allira took a moment to admire the body he'd been given and liked what she saw. She liked it even more when he started to disrobe. He shrugged out of his cloak and unbuckled his belt before he noticed her staring.

"Am I doing this alone, or will you be joining me?" He raised an eyebrow.

She smirked and crossed her arms over her chest. "Oh, I'll join you, but I want to see what I'm in for first."

He laughed. "I'd twirl for your perusal, but I can't stand up in the tent." He still peeled his doublet over his head and set it to the side.

Her mouth went dry. She'd seen plenty of male bodies throughout her life, but something about Josten's just ticked all her boxes. He had powerful shoulders and a broad chest with dark hair narrowing down to a line across his belly. While the muscles weren't defined, he didn't carry much fat over them. Trim hips gave way to powerful thighs which came into view along with his cock and balls when he shucked his pants. The line of hair spread over his groin and his swelling shaft rose to catch her attention as he settled, naked, on her bedding.

After a moment, Josten snorted. "Are you going to join me, or are you simply going to let me sit naked on your bed in a blustery day?"

Allira blinked. "Oh! Nope, but I was enjoying the general splendor of the view."

He grinned. "I'd like to do the same."

She'd rarely felt self-conscious of her body—in combat, there wasn't time to waste on one's physical appearance—but she hadn't been with anyone in an intimate aspect in a long time. Baring her body felt a lot like baring her soul to him. She grimaced as she unbuttoned her pants.

Josten's hand landed on her arm. "What's wrong?"

"Hm? Oh, nothing. I'm fine."

"Your expression says otherwise. Are you no longer interested?"

"Oh, glory! No, nothing like that." She met his gaze. "It's just been a long time since I've been with anyone."

He tilted his head, his body relaxed despite his nakedness. "I can guarantee it's been longer for me."

She blinked and laughed. "Yeah, I guess that's true."

He gently squeezed her arm. "What's bothering you? Are you cold?"

"No—well, yeah, a little, but mostly I'm not used to being intimate... with anyone."

He tilted his head, and a warm smile curled his lips. "Perhaps I can help with that."

She raised an eyebrow. "How?"

"Let me undress you. It gives you a chance to let go of your worries and me a chance to get some practice in." He ran his hand down to hers and trailed his fingers over her palm. "Do you trust me to treat you with reverence?"

She tilted her head. "Just as long as you don't treat me like I'll break. I'm not that fragile."

He grunted. "The word fragile doesn't apply to you." He pulled off her belt. "Hell, I think the other humans were more fragile than you."

He drew her pants down her legs, exposing the skin, before pulling them off and laying them to the side. When he turned back, he stroked his warm hands up the outside of her legs, leaving tingles in his wake. His fingers curled around her under garments and tugged them down as well, exposing her core to the cool air.

She expected him to pause and spend time enjoying her pussy, but he moved on almost immediately to finish removing her clothes. She shivered a little as her cloak and shirt came off, and her nipples tightened into little peaks with exposure.

"So beautiful." Josten's words came out in a whisper, and he leaned over her to take one nipple into his mouth.

Allira gasped at the hot, slick grip of his lips on her nipple and thrust her chest out as his hand closed on the neglected breast with a gentle squeeze. He hummed against her first breast before releasing the nipple and moving to the other. He suckled for a moment, sending pulses of pleasure straight to her pussy, and her juices coated her inner thighs from arousal.

She had no idea her breasts were so sensitive, but she didn't want him to stop.

He released her breast with his free hand and trailed it down her body until his fingers swept over her mound to stroke her vulva. He worked his fingers into her folds and groaned when he found her wet.

"Oh, Allira, you're so wet for me. So damn tempting." He pulled back from her breast and dropped his gaze to his hand. "With your permission, I need to taste you."

Her arousal pulled back a bit, and she blinked. "You want to taste me?"

He nodded as he slid down her body, dropping to his belly. "Here. I need to taste you here." He levered her knees over his shoulders and positioned his face right at her groin. "May I?"

She swallowed hard. "Yes."

His hot breath teased the hairs on her vulva before something hot and wet pierced her folds. She realized it was his tongue when it teased her clit and sent delicious spears of pleasure through her at each stroke. At first, he used light, teasing touches to spur her arousal to greater heights. Then he sealed his whole mouth over her slit and feasted on her core.

Allira fell into the pulses of sensation from his beard and tongue caressing her sensitive flesh, whimpering in time with his strokes. Josten hummed against her labia, as if he found great satisfaction in licking her core. He teased her slit with his tongue, but she soon felt a harder intrusion with a rough surface. When it curled inside her, stroking that special spot, she recognized his callused finger.

"Oh, glory, Joss. Yes, there. Right there."

She rocked her hips against his face and his finger, and he obligingly rubbed harder on her spot. Her orgasm built with startling speed, and she grabbed his head to hold him where she needed him most. He licked and stroked her with relentless gentleness, and she feared he'd hold her release just out of reach until he sucked on her clit.

Her orgasm detonated through her and she wailed her release, flying harder and higher than she had in years. Pleasure shot through her as he kept licking and sucking on her core, and she rode the high as long as she could.

When she finally came back to herself and relaxed her legs, Josten pulled back and wiped his mouth with his hand, a smirk curling his lips.

"You taste delightful, my lady."

Allira chuckled. "If you say so. I'll take your word for it."

"I'm happy to prove it to you again, if you're interested." The smirk widened into a grin.

She moaned. "In a moment. Right now, I just want to bask in this."

He chuckled and crawled up beside her. "Bask all you like. I'm in no hurry."

She glanced down at his raging hard-on and raised an eyebrow. "Are you sure? Because I can help you with that."

"I'm hoping you will, but whenever you're ready. I'm enjoying watching your euphoria."

She let her eyes close and a smile curl her lips. "That's a good word for it. Euphoria." She sighed and opened her eyes. "I'm gonna need more of that."

"As you command, my lady." He started to get up, but she held him back with a hand on his chest.

"Nope, this time I want your cock." She sat up and pushed his shoulders back into the bedding.

His eyebrows went up. "What do you have in mind?"

"I've always wanted to know what it's like to ride a king. Do you happen to know one who needs to be ridden?" She grinned at him as she straddled his thighs. "I assure you, I'm an excellent rider."

"Are you now?" His smile made his eyes dance. "I think you should show me what you've got—prove to me you can handle this kind of royal mount."

"As the king commands." She winked before she dipped her hips and rubbed her vulva against his hard shaft.

Josten moaned and rocked his hips, grinding his cock against her clit. She whimpered and rolled her hips to find the delicious friction that sent more cream to her pussy. He gripped her hips to hold her steady as they rocked together, his eyes full of arousal. But it wasn't enough.

"I need you, Josten."

"I'm here. Take my cock and ride it, bright star."

She blinked at the endearment, but she didn't have to be told twice. She gripped his hard shaft slick from her juices, and fit it to her entrance. She met his gaze as she slid slowly down his rigid cock until he was seated all the way to the hilt.

"Oh glory, Joss. You're so thick." The intrusion of his cock felt both huge and perfect. He filled her completely, and she needed a few moments to revel in his sexual perfection.

"And you're so tight, bright star. So perfectly tight."

"Only for you, my iron king." She met his gaze and rocked her hips as she squeezed his shaft with her inner muscles. "You're mine, Josten. My iron king."

"Yeeessssss." He gripped her hips and pulled out only to power back inside her. "Ride me, Allira. Drive us both to ecstasy."

She didn't have to be told twice. She braced her hands on either side of his head as she rocked herself off his cock, dragging it along her clit. Then she sat back down on the hard intrusion, ratcheting up the friction. They both moaned, and Allira saw stars when his cock came to rest against her special spot.

She rose up and did it again, reveling in the pleasure she felt with him between her legs. She'd imagined making love to Josten and she'd endured a particularly hot dream, but nothing compared to having his cock sliding in and out of her wet pussy. Each stroke of his shaft brought greater pleasure, building up her orgasm with inexorable progress.

Josten watched her with an intense gaze, rocking his hips each time she came down. It was sexy as hell, but when he took a nipple into his mouth while she rode him, unexpected excitement crashed through her with the wet heat on her breast. She whimpered and rocked a little harder on his cock.

She'd started out slow, enjoying the slide and burn of sexual friction, but as her arousal built, so did her desperation. She increased the frequency of her thrusts, and soon she rode her iron king in an intense lope, slamming down on his hips as she ground her clit against his shaft.

"Oh yes, Josten. I need you. I need you so much." She ground her hips harder, and he slammed up into her pussy, hitting just the right spot.

"Oh yes, yes, yes!"

"Ride me so hard, bright star! Yes!"

Her orgasm tore through her, taking hold of her body and moving it while she flew into ecstasy. Josten roared and slammed her hips down onto his a few more times as hot cum shot into her. He held her steady as her orgasm let her sail away into bliss before gently letting her return to her cozy tent and the hot, out-of-breath man between her legs.

He's not the only one out of breath.

She laughed a little as she let her gaze rest on his beautiful, bearded face. "Better than my fantasies, Joss."

The edge of his mouth quirked upwards. "Better than mine, too."

"Oh yeah? I didn't know ghosts could have fantasies, being phantoms." She grinned.

"Yeah, I never really got the hang of that." He reached up to caress her face. "But I certainly enjoyed my time haunting you." He paused a moment, searching her face for something. "I love you, Allira."

Tear sprang to her eyes, and she swallowed hard to find her voice. "I love you, too. I don't think I realized how much until it seemed like you'd forgotten me and I had to think of what I'd do without you in my life."

He grimaced as she pulled off him and settled at his side. "I'm sorry about that. I suspect Mectarn will give me hell over it for a few months or years as a reminder."

Allira snorted. "That sounds like something she'd do to keep you humble."

"She often reminded me that being a king meant more than riches and servants. It meant standing up and protecting my people. The denizens of the Caverns all became my people." He met her gaze. "Which is why I think the Council of Elders will agree to let us stay here together."

She rolled over to look him in the eyes. "Are you sure that's what you want? I mean, it's what *I* want, but maybe you're ready to rejoin the living."

Josten snorted. "If humans are anything like the men you came with, I'd rather live with the Goblins."

"Harsh, but fair." She smiled to take the sting out of her words. "But if we do stay—and they allow us—we're going to need to make this more than just a temporary camp to survive the winter. I'm thinking a three-room house, at least, with a wide deck around the fire pit, and a real barn for the horses."

"Once we talk to the Council of Elders about staying—"

"If they agree—"

"*When* they agree, I'll ask Gundri and the Orcs to help with the construction. I'm sure they'd be willing. Gundri already likes you, and with Mectarn's blessing, the others won't have any reservations."

Allira rolled her eyes. "You're making a lot of assumptions about the Goblins and Orcs."

"I know them, Allira. Don't worry." Josten gave her a warm smile. "It's going to work out great." He squeezed her hips. "Now, perhaps we should try to find something to eat. I'm famished."

She sighed but her heart swelled. "Yeah, okay. Gotta feed you somehow. Let's get dressed and visit our neighbors. They might have something you can feast on."

"I'm more than happy to feast on you again, my dear." He shot her a smoldering look as they redressed.

"Very tempting, my iron king, but only after we've settled our future a bit." She pulled her shirt over her head and yanked on her pants. "Then I might feast on you, as well."

Josten buckled his belt over his doublet and settled his cloak on his shoulders as he grinned. "Now that I'm definitely looking forward to experiencing."

She laughed. "Get your boots on and let's go find breakfast. We can talk about sexual feasting later."

"Aw, you're no fun."

But his grin remained as he laced his boots, and they headed back to the Dreadstone Caverns hand-in-hand. Allira didn't mind the rain now that her world had brightened. With Josten at her side, she had hope and peace for the first time in her life, and she would fight to keep it forever.

Epilogue

THREE MONTHS LATER

Allira took a deep breath and let it out slowly as the town of Capstone Creek came into view.

I didn't think I'd ever see this place again.

She had mixed feelings about returning, but she didn't want her grandmothers to worry unnecessarily. She glanced over at Josten seated beside her in a cloak and leather gloves, and he gave her a warm and encouraging smile.

Being hand-fasted by a Goblin shaman will do that.

They'd spoken to the Council of Elders, and while there was some trepidation about having a human in close proximity, the council agreed that Allira had been an ally and an asset during the time of the latest invasion. Coupled with Josten's and Mectarn's endorsements, they'd agreed to let her stay in her little estate outside the Dreadstone Caverns. Gundri, Crent, and Tral volunteered to help build a true house with the deck both she and Josten had envisioned.

When Josten announced they were to be married, the Goblins and Orcs set up a great party, and they were hand-fasted under the light of the full moon gilding everyone's shoulders. Mectarn had been healed enough to conduct the ceremony and blessed their union, giving them a three-month trial period before the bond became official.

And something did feel different between them now that the deadline had passed. Oh sure, they'd been living together in their newly constructed house in the lea of the Dreadstone Hills, but knowing they'd weathered the probationary period settled something deep inside her. Not that she'd had any doubts about Josten, or his love, but now it was official.

"This is a bustling city. I didn't expect it to be so large." Josten's voice broke into her musings.

Allira snorted. "You saw Riven Fell. Capstone Creek is smaller."

Josten grunted. "Too many humans for me. I'm just grateful they don't find anything useful about the Flamewood Forest or they'd overrun the Dreadstone Caverns with their numbers."

She had to admit she agreed. Now she just had to convince the humans to stop their stupid festival and they'd be safe. She snorted. When it came to gold and riches, not much stopped humans beyond threats and violence. She sighed and tightened her cloak around her as the rain sheeted down over them.

The weather had turned cold and it had taken them more than two weeks to travel to the human habitation. She'd turned them toward the river to make the traveling easier, but it took them well off the straight path to Capstone Creek. Josten mentioned he preferred the solitude to the bustling human settlements, and she suspected it was because of his decades of solitude. She hadn't minded staying away from humans on the trip.

"Humans are disgusting." He gestured to the crowded streets with shops and homes.

Allira laughed. "You are one, now."

"Yeah, that's disappointing as hell, but at least I've learned from my worst mistakes."

Allira raised an eyebrow. "And how long did that take you?"

He didn't answer as they arrived at the gates to the Magistrate's Estate. She'd puzzled over who she should talk to first, but ultimately decided the Magistrate of Capstone Creek would be the one with the power to stop the Festival of the Relic. She hauled on the reins to stop the horses and nodded to the guards.

"Knight Maplestaff returning from the Dreadstone Tombs with a message for the Magistrate."

The guards' suspicious expressions shifted into disbelief. "No one ever comes back from the Tombs. How do we believe it's really you?"

Allira shot them a flat look as she opened her cloak. "If you don't recognize my colors, call the Magistrate and the Town Council. They should be notified anyway, but I doubt they want to come out here to the front gates to hear the information I have. Of course, if you're secure enough in your positions to endure their displeasure when they learn you kept me out here waiting, go ahead. Either way, they'll want to hear what I have to say."

There was some discussion, but Allira sat quietly with Josten, waiting for someone to either get the Magistrate or make a decision about her claim. It helped that she wore her knight's colors and the helm she'd taken with her to the Tombs.

At last, a man was sent back into town, and they were allowed through the gate into the main courtyard of the estate. It used to hold gardens when her grandmothers had settled in Capstone Creek, but the current magistrate had removed all the vegetation and paved the courtyard with flat bricks. It made the area seem stark and bleak.

How fitting for a guy who sends men to die at the Tombs.

They rolled to a stop in the windswept courtyard and sat for a few minutes, waiting for someone to come. No one spoke for a while, and Allira wondered if the Magistrate would let them stew out in the blustery day.

Josten surveyed the courtyard and mansion with cool eyes. "He thinks a lot of himself, doesn't he?"

Allira snorted. "I'm sure he does, but he inherited this place from the previous man in charge. I don't know who decided the Magistrate needed a huge house just for one man, but there you go. Hell, you ended up with an entire cave system, so I'm not sure you have room to talk."

"Good point." He grinned ruefully. "But at least I had room-mates."

Allira laughed, and her peel of laughter rang against the rain-washed stone of the courtyard, making the guards jump. They resettled as the doors to the mansion opened and a small entourage came out into the courtyard.

"Who are you?"

Allira remembered the magistrate. He was a balding man with a slight paunch that still cut an impressive figure. He wore long robes edged with satin and a thick cloak made of fur that gave the impression he stood larger than everyone else. But his expression was cold and forbidding under his matching fur hat.

"Knight Allira Maplestaff, last of the living knights from the Festival of the Relic."

The Magistrate's eyes opened wide, and he took in her colors as well as the man seated beside her, as if calculating the veracity of her claim.

"It cannot be. No one survived this year's Festival."

She snorted. "No one but me. I've brought the fallen knights' colors to be returned to their families so they know what became of them." She gestured to the wagon. "I have them here as proof."

"Show us."

She nodded to Josten, and he jumped down to pull back the tarp covering the wagon. The knights' colors were folded neatly in groups along with their gear and a few broken weapons. The undamaged weapons had remained with the Goblins as trophies for future defense. Josten dropped the tarp and crossed his arms over his chest as Allira took in the Magistrate's reaction.

The man surveyed the contents, then dismissed them as unimportant as he returned his gaze to hers.

"Why are you here?"

She just stared at him a moment. Was he serious? He didn't react, so she cleared her throat.

"I'll make this brief, Magistrate." Allira jumped down from her perch on the wagon's seat and wandered around to the back. She rested her hand on the tarp. "*These* are the possessions of the latest crop of knights you sent with me to the Dreadstone Tombs. You remember, the guys I was coerced to go with four months ago? I brought their gear back for their families so you can give them their rewards for going on this year's suicide mission." She gestured to the gear and colors.

The Magistrate stared at the wagon without moving or directing others to retrieve the items. The silence stretched, and Allira flattened her expression.

"Are you going to uphold your end of the deal for the families of the fallen?" She raised her eyebrows as Josten casually let his arms drop. She hoped they wouldn't have to fight the guards, but her earlier thought came back to her.

Not much influenced humans beyond riches, threats, or violence.

"There were no deals made with the others, only you." The Magistrate's mouth twisted in distaste.

Allira nodded. "Our deal still stands, then? My grandmothers' farm's taxes are paid in perpetuity until such time as they choose to sell or pass on?"

The Magistrate inclined his head. "Of course."

"Good. I'd like to see the document that's written on and I need two copies—one for me, and one for my grandmothers." Allira nodded with a confident smile.

"Document?" The Magistrate's jaw dropped.

"Yes, I want to be sure all parties are still in agreement." Her smile brightened, but her eyes did not. "I don't want there to be any question of my grandmothers' taxes come the spring."

"Knight Maplestaff, you don't trust us to keep our word?"

"Not in the very least, Magistrate," Allira replied cheerfully. "Go have a scribe return with my documents and I'll leave you the gear to distribute as you see fit. Also, you can let the princess off the hook. She doesn't have to marry anyone. I'm not interested in her land or titles."

The Magistrate shot her a dry look as if that was a given, but he didn't say it aloud.

"And finally, the Festival of the Relic ends now. Don't send anyone back to the Dreadstone Tombs. There's no treasure there to find."

The Magistrate raised his chin. "This is because you've claimed it for yourself, I presume?"

"Sort of. The Dreadstone Tombs are under my protection, but there's no treasure. There never was."

"How can we be sure you're telling the truth? You could be keeping it all for yourself." The Magistrate narrowed his eyes with a shrewd look.

And this is exactly why I want your deal in writing.

Allira nodded. "It doesn't surprise me that you think that way. I'm sure that's what you would do given the chance. Look around, Magistrate. Do you see anyone else here who's been to the Tombs and survived? I'm the only one among you who has been inside. There's no treasure. There's no gold. And the only Relic from the Dreadstone King is a crumbling skeleton on a stone throne." She gestured to Josten with one hand. "He can verify, if you don't believe me. But I'm not sure a man who's lived near the Tombs for decades could make you believe, either."

The Magistrate fixed Josten with a gimlet eye. "And who are you?"

"My name is Josten Ironheart."

When he said nothing else, Allira had to rub her nose to hide her smirk. Josten could do stoic like no one else. Except for maybe Tral when he didn't understand Allira's humor.

The Magistrate scowled. "And you've lived near the Dreadstone Tombs for decades?"

Josten nodded. "I have."

"Do you agree with Knight Maplestaff that there is no treasure or Relic?"

"Not in all the time I've lived there." Which was technically true. He'd been dead for more than seventy years and only living for the last few weeks, and the Iron Crown was buried in the deepest hole in the Dreadstone Caverns. "They're just caves with ruins of an old kingdom, and debris like this." He waved at the colors and gear in the wagon. "There's no magical Relic or treasure left over from the Dreadstone King's reign. It's all empty lies told by wandering minstrels or bards."

"Then who kills the knights who go each year?" The Magistrate pointed at the gear that Allira slowly unloaded from the wagon.

"You didn't think the Tombs were empty, did you?" She shook her head as she dropped Swindell's armor and saddle colors onto the brick courtyard. "There *are* people there, and they defend their homes from the barbaric invaders. They are murdered by the men you send." She dropped Argyle's and Danville's gear on the ground and straightened. "This 'festival' ends now. Don't send anyone else. There's nothing to find except people living their lives."

"Why should we believe you? How do we know *you* didn't claim the Relic for yourself?" The Magistrate straightened and looked down his nose at her.

Allira snorted. "I told you, Magistrate, there is no treasure and no Relic—if there was once, it's long gone. People live in the caves now, and they aren't hiding treasure. They're just trying to make lives." She pointed at the Magistrate. "There's nothing for anyone to find, and the Dreadstone Tombs are now under my protection. If you ignore my warning and keep sending people to the Tombs, they will be turned away. If they persist, they will pay fees to be determined by the damage done, and sent on their way. But if they keep trying to get in through violence..." She glanced at Josten. "The Tombs are guarded by a fierce skeletal warrior who cannot die and cannot be defeated. The last group of knights awakened it and it decimated them when they wouldn't stop. *That's* who's been killing the invaders."

The Magistrate scoffed. "Children's stories to frighten away the weak."

"Remember who you're talking to, Magistrate. *I'm* the only one who's been there and seen the monster who dwells within." Allira hardened her voice. "It only rises when the invaders can't be reasoned with. Anyone who comes to the Dreadstone Hills in peace to trade and treat with the peoples therein will be left alone. But those who come with violent intent will be treated with violence."

"So you say. How do we know you don't now live in riches beyond your dreams?"

Allira just laughed. "Do I look like I'm living in riches? And my dreams aren't gilded in gold and jewels, Magistrate. They're about peace and community. Leave the Dreadstone Tombs to their memories and return the knights' gear to their families."

Allira settled in the back of her empty wagon and crossed her arms over her chest.

"What are you doing?" The Magistrate's lip curled.

"I'm waiting for my documents and then I'll be on my way."

"You may be waiting a long time. There will be no documents coming to you today." The Magistrate turned to leave.

"So, you would let it be known that you don't deal fairly with people?" Josten's voice rang with scorn across the courtyard as he narrowed his eyes. "I can't say I'm surprised. Knight Maplestaff said you were honorable and would uphold any agreements made. But I can see she was mistaken."

Allira shivered. Josten had been a king, and his voice rang with authority. The guards shifted nervously, shooting looks between Josten and the Magistrate. Even the man himself looked uneasy.

They waited for the man to respond, but when he didn't, Josten's expression grew cold and remote. "Very well. We'll spread the word far and wide that the Magistrate of Capstone Creek is dishonest, reneges on deals made in good faith, and lies about prizes and treasures given." He nodded to Allira, and she hopped down from the back. He waved at the other guards. "Load this back up, boys."

Allira shook her head. "I guess I should've talked to the Town Council instead of you. I'm sure they have a list of the families of the fallen. I think Dinsmoore was from Riven Fell, right? And his family is pretty prominent. I'm sure they'll be interested to know what happened and how he was treated by the Magistrate of Capstone Creek. I'll be happy to let them know their son died for nothing."

At first, the Magistrate sneered, as only one of guards moved to help reload all the gear on the brick pavers. But his expression changed to unease as more joined their fellow, their faces filled with loathing and disgust. They picked up the gear and colors with careful reverence and placed them back in the wagon.

Allira smiled inwardly. *Don't mess with or deride people's heroes.*

"And who are you to speak thus?"

"Me? I'm just the Keeper of the Flamewood Forest, liaison between the humans and the people of the Dreadstone Hills." Josten shrugged as another carriage trundled into the courtyard. "But

I won't be dealing with you. I might strike up a deal with the Magistrate of Riven Fell. I believe we traveled through there on our way here, right?"

Allira nodded. "Yup. Nice town. Big shipping port." She closed the back of the wagon and resecured the tarp. "Still need those documents, Magistrate."

"Which documents?" An officious-looking man in a wool cloak and wire-rimmed glasses bustled up from the newly arrived carriage. Allira offered him a smile.

"Mayor Lindquist, you didn't need to come all this way." The Magistrate scowled.

"I understand one of the Knights from the Festival has actually returned. Why wouldn't we come for this joyous occasion?" Lindquist waved at the rest of the town council members as they disembarked from the carriage. "Knight Maplestaff! You've returned. Huzzah!"

There were other cheers from the rest of the council as the Magistrate's jaw dropped.

"You recognize this woman?"

The mayor's eyebrows went up. "Of course. She was the knight you convinced to go with the others in exchange for paying taxes on her family farm. I'm delighted to see you've survived, Maplestaff. Have you come to claim the prizes?"

"No, Mayor. I'm just here to deliver the fallen knights' gear and retrieve the contract showing that my farm is cared for in perpetuity. You do have that document?"

"Of course, of course. We honor our agreements." Lindquist nodded, and Allira made a note to only talk to him from now on.

"She claims there is no relic to be recovered at the Tombs." The Magistrate waved at her with derision. "An obvious fabrication."

"No relic, you say? Is this true?" Lindquist turned to Allira.

"It is. The Dreadstone Tombs are filled with people and children, not riches or a magical artifact. The knights have been deceived by fairytales."

"I'd like to hear more of this in the Town Hall, if you're willing, Knight Maplestaff."

The Magistrate gaped. "You believe her?"

"You don't? How surprising." Lindquist's voice flattened before he looked at the wagon. "Is this the gear of the fallen?"

"Yes, Mayor." Josten lifted the tarp to expose the reloaded gear. "The Magistrate didn't seem interested in returning it to the families of the fallen."

"He didn't, did he?" Lindquist swung his disapproving scowl on the Magistrate. "Well, we wouldn't want to bother *his lordship* with such trivial things as remembering the dead or their families."

The Magistrate stiffened as the guards around him looked at each other.

"Now then, since you've come all this way, perhaps you would accompany us back to the Town Hall where we can sort all this out, give you what prizes you're due, and yes, the documents showing the deal you made with Capstone Creek during the Festival of the Relic." Lindquist waved toward the gate of the estate. "I'm sure you'll be more comfortable there, anyway. We at least can offer you a meal and warm tea."

Allira beamed at the mayor. "We'd be delighted, Mayor Lindquist. How's your mom, by the way? Has her arthritis improved?"

"Oh, you know, the winter is coming and with it the damp. It makes it harder for her to get a good night's rest. Thank you for asking. But we can talk more once we get out of this weather." He gave an exaggerated shiver and gestured to his carriage. "If you'll follow us into the Town Square, we can get everything sorted."

"Sounds good, Mayor."

Josten climbed up beside Allira and settled his cloak over them both, his hand on his dagger in case the guards tried anything. She turned the wagon slowly so she didn't run anyone over and Josten kept an eye on the Magistrate as they drove away. Lindquist waved as he climbed into his carriage with the other members of the council, and they all headed out of the gates toward the town center.

"Do you think the Mayor will uphold your contract?" Josten nodded toward the mayor's carriage as they rumbled over the cobbles outside the estate.

"Oh, I know he will. Lindquist was the one who recommended me to the Magistrate. He's my Mima's best friend from when they were kids, and he's been honest to a fault." Allira grinned. "I believe he presided over Nanna and Mima's wedding."

"So why didn't you go to the Town Hall to begin with?"

"The Magistrate has the final say about who goes on the team for the Festival and which prizes are bestowed." Allira shrugged. "I figured he'd be the one to have the contract and want to contact the families. Had I known just how big a jackass he'd be, I would've visited with Lindquist first."

"I think Lindquist is the one we should negotiate with from now on. The Magistrate can rot all by himself in his estate." Josten shook his head. "He reminds me of me, and that's not a good thing. He's gonna end up all alone and paranoid, and for what? Fleeting power?" He snorted. "It's an illusion based on others agreeing to it. And when they stop agreeing?" He shook his head again. "It all comes down around your ears."

"It just might for the Magistrate, but we won't be here to see it. He can keep his power. I just want my document and to get rid of this gear. Then I'm going back to my little cabin beside the Hills with my husband." That gave her a little thrill.

Josten grinned. "Almost-husband. Mectarn says the trial period is almost up."

"She said that when we left. By the time we get back, it'll be official, but I still want the party." Allira raised her chin. "Besides, we have to start putting together the promotional materials for that warhorsey riding thing. You know, for Goblin and Orc kids' birthdays."

Josten barked a laugh. "You still want to do that?"

"Why not? It would give us good practice for when our own kids come along."

"What?" He shot a look at her flat belly. "Is there something I need to know?"

Allira flashed a smirk. "No, not yet. I'm just keeping it in mind because I plan on riding my iron king bareback as much as possible." She gave him a saucy wink.

He reached over and squeezed her hip. "The moment we're truly alone, I'll be happy to give you a ride, bright star."

She grinned and nodded before something occurred to her. "Hey, what was that title you gave yourself? The Keeper of Flamewood Forest? Very impressive. What made you think of that?"

Josten shrugged. "Men like the Magistrate don't respect anyone unless they have titles. He wouldn't take me seriously unless he thought I had some rank. I figured he'd listen to someone who lives in a scary place like Flamewood. Besides, I *used* to be the Dreadstone King—I figure Keeper of the Flamewood is only a small step down."

She laughed as they rolled through the town, people hiding under the eaves from the rain.

"Can't argue with that, and it sounds mysterious as hell. That totally fits." She shot him a look. "What does that make me?"

He leaned close until his breath tickled her ear. "That makes you come until you're breathless. But if you're asking about titles... I'd say you're the Guardian of the Dreadstone Caverns. Unless you want to stay the Dismemberer of Dreadstone."

"No, I'm good with Guardian of Dreadstone."

Joy spread through her at both his naughty words and the new title. She liked the idea of being the Guardian of Dreadstone. It gave her purpose without the violence she'd lived with for much of her adult life. She could use her skills for protection rather than destruction. As they rumbled their way toward the Town Hall, a real future spread out ahead of her and she would face it with the man who captured her heart, the Dreadstone King.

THE END

About Siobhan Muir

Siobhan Muir lives in Cheyenne, Wyoming, with her husband, two daughters, a house panther, and a very patient dog. When not writing, she can be found looking down a microscope at fossil fox teeth, pursuing her other love, paleontology. An avid reader of science fiction/fantasy, her husband gave her a paranormal romance for Christmas one year, and she was hooked for good.

In previous lives, Siobhan has been an actor at the Colorado Renaissance Festival, a field geologist in the Aleutian Islands, and restored inter-planetary imagery at the USGS. She's hiked to the top of Mount St. Helens and to the bottom of Meteor Crater.

Siobhan writes kick-ass adventure with hot sex for men and women to enjoy. She believes in happily ever after, redemption, and communication, all of which you will find in her paranormal and dauntless romance stories.

Connect with Siobhan online at:
https://siobhanmuir.com/
Facebook
Instagram
Siobhan's Blog
Tumblr
Bluesky
Mastodon
MeWe

Patreon

Or sign up for her newsletter to get excerpts and cover reveals and other fun extras.

NEWSLETTER

Other Books by Siobhan Muir

Her Devoted Vampire
The Sorceress of Song and Flame
Mr. Fixit's Billionaire
Fossil Beds Bed & Breakfast
The Dreadstone King

Bad Boys of Beta Squad Series
Bronco's Rough Ride
The Navy's Ghost
Rimshot's Hard Target
Bam-Bam's Inked Hart
Deli's Take Out

Callowwood Pack Series
Queen Bitch of the Callowwood Pack
The Callowwood Canine Caper

Cloudburst Colorado Series
A Hell Hound's Fire
The Beltane Witch
Christmas I.C.E. Magic
Cloudburst Ice Magic
Cloudburst Coffee & Spa

Courting the Dragon Widow
The Samhain Soldier

Concrete Angels MC Series
My Forever Cocky Biker Encounter
Dude With a Cool Car
Angel Ink
The Concrete Angel
Running From the Texas Millionaire

Elemental Hearts Series
Wildfire's Heart
A Timeless Heart

Rifts Series
Take the Reins
A Centaur's Solstice Wish
In Death's Shadow

Silver State Mysteries Series
Second Chance Succubus

Summit Springs Sapphic Romance
Broken Chains
In Plain Sight

Triple Star Ranch Series

Rope a Falling Star
Star Light, Star Bright
Star Spangled Banner

Ultimate Recon Series
Darwin's Evolution

Warbler Peninsula Series
Order of the Dragon
The Valkyrie's Sword
Burning Yuletide

The Ivory Road Serial
A Walk in the Sand
Outback Dreams
A Dance Between Worlds
The Karobis Calls

Coming Soon
The Siren Queen (Sirens, Inc. #1)
The Siren and the Scientist (Sirens, Inc. #2)